La Shun L. Carroll is a Lifetime Member of American MENSA and full member of Sigma Xi, the Scientific Research Honor Society. He was awarded the Arthur Schomburg Fellowship to pursue graduate studies maintaining it for four consecutive years until receiving his doctoral degree, graduating Cum Laude, from the University at Buffalo School of Dental Medicine. Subsequently, Dr. Carroll earned his Ed.M. graduate degree specializing in Science and the Public from the University at Buffalo Graduate School of Education. Research interests include metaphysics, logic, science, technology, and education. Non-research interests include writing, illustrating, music, and learning in general. Dr. Carroll was an Adjunct Professor in the Department of Biological Sciences at Saint Michael's College in Vermont.

As an undergraduate, Dr. Carroll graduated #1 with a B.A. degree, Magna Cum Laude, from Baruch College, CUNY, majoring in both Philosophy and Natural Science. His scholarly publications include "Theoretical Biomimetics: A biological design-driven concept for creative problem-solving as applied to the optimal sequencing of active learning techniques in educational theory" in the Multidisciplinary Journal for Education, Social and Technological Sciences (October 2017), "Fundamentals of Logic, Reasoning, and Argumentation" also in the Multidisciplinary Journal for Education, Social and Technological Sciences (April 2020), "Concerning the Ethics of Justice, Care, and Personal

Responsibility as a Framework for Criteria Selection in Transplant Recipients" published in The Integral Review (October 2023), "The Conceptual Access-NeTwORk (CANTOR) Thesis: Theorizing the Development or Success of New Internet-Based Products, Services, or Technologies" in the Indonesian Journal of Innovation and Applied Sciences (June 2023), a paper entitled "Unbearable Suffering Obviates Euthanasia: Definitionally-Derived Set of Propositions Comprising the Purpose, Claim, and Benefit Lead to Contradiction Establishing the Paradox of Euthanasia" in History and Philosophy of Medicine (History and Philosophy of Medicine 2022), and a highly cited influential paper entitled "A Comprehensive Definition of Technology from an Ethological Perspective" (MDPI, 2017).

This book is dedicated to Adelaide Elizabeth.

La Shun L. Carroll

CHOSEN

AUSTIN MACAULEY PUBLISHERS™

LONDON · CAMBRIDGE · NEW YORK · SHARJAH

Ordering Information
Quantity sales: Special discounts are available on quantity purchases by corporations, associations, and others. For details, contact the publisher at the address below.

Publisher's Cataloging-in-Publication data
Carroll, La Shun L.
Chosen

ISBN 9798886937695 (Paperback)
ISBN 9798886937701 (ePub e-book)

Library of Congress Control Number: 2024908150

www.austinmacauley.com/us

First Published 2024
Austin Macauley Publishers LLC
40 Wall Street, 33rd Floor, Suite 3302
New York, NY 10005
USA

mail-usa@austinmacauley.com
+1 (646) 5125767

I would like to thank Baby, Ashes, Reagan, and Taz—the late sister-feline muses who were by my side for nearly two decades during my creative scholarly and literary endeavors. I miss you.

In addition, I wish to thank my late mother, Marggio Carroll and grandmother, Ellen Carroll, for everything that they sacrificed for me to be in the position I am. I can never repay you.

Chapter 1

The sun filtered through the leaves of the towering oak tree, casting dappled light over the meticulously maintained lawn of the Thompson residence. Ted Thompson lounged on the porch swing, a satisfied smile playing across his face as he gazed out at the small-town charm of Greenfield.

"Ted, can you give me a hand with these groceries?" Susan Thompson called from inside the house. The screen door creaked open as she emerged with her arms laden with bags.

"Of course," Ted replied, springing up from the swing and rushing to assist her. They carried the bags into the kitchen where David Thompson was already unpacking more items.

"Thanks, son," David said, flashing Ted a warm smile. "You're always so willing to help out around here."

"Hey, it's the least I can do," Ted said, returning his father's smile. "You have given me such an incredible life."

As Ted continued to help with the groceries, his thoughts wandered to how grateful he was for the stable upbringing his adoptive parents had provided. He could not imagine a life without their unwavering support and guidance. While some of his friends struggled within broken homes and chaotic environments, he found solace in the predictability and comfort that the Thompson household offered.

"Your father and I just wanted you to have the best possible start in life," Susan said softly, placing a gentle hand on Ted's shoulder. "We know it wasn't easy for you when you first came to us, but we always believed you were meant to be part of our family."

"Thank you," Ted replied, his eyes glistening with unshed tears. "I do not know where I'd be without you and Dad. You've made my life better than I could have ever dreamed."

"Always remember, Ted, that no matter where life takes you, this will always be your home," David added, wrapping his arm around Ted's shoulders. "We're so proud of the man you've become."

"Thanks, Dad," Ted murmured, feeling a swell of pride and gratitude wash over him. He knew he was incredibly fortunate to have found such a loving and nurturing family in the Thompsons. And as he stood there, sandwiched between his adoptive parents in their cozy kitchen, he could not help but feel an immense sense of contentment with the life they'd built together.

Ted stood in front of the full-length mirror in his bedroom, smoothing out the wrinkles on his freshly pressed shirt. His short, dark hair was neatly combed to one side, accentuating his strong jawline, and piercing blue eyes. He straightened his tie with a satisfied smile, admiring his athletic build and polished appearance.

"Looking good, Ted," he said to himself, giving a small wink before stepping back from the mirror. There was no denying that he carried himself with an air of confidence and poise that set him apart from others his age. It was yet another testament to the nurturing environment provided by his adoptive parents.

As he walked down the stairs, thoughts of his birth family occasionally flitted through his mind. He knew very little about them, but he couldn't help but wonder if there was someone out there who shared his same striking features and easygoing charm.

"Chosen! Get your butt in here, we're gonna be late!" Melissa called from the living room, her voice tinged with both exasperation and affection.

"Coming, Mom!" Chosen hollered back, quickly tying his worn sneakers, and grabbing his threadbare jacket. Much like Ted, Chosen had short, dark hair and an athletic build—a fact unbeknownst to either sibling. However, unlike his twin brother, Chosen's clothes were noticeably well-worn, a visual reminder of the financial struggles he and his mother faced in their small Brooksville apartment.

"Alright, I'm ready," Chosen announced as he emerged from his cramped bedroom, trying to suppress a yawn. Despite the hardships they faced, he loved his life with Melissa and would not trade it for anything.

"Good, now let's get going," Melissa replied with a soft smile, her wavy brown hair framing her warm, kind eyes. "I don't want you to be late for your job interview."

"Thanks, Mom," Chosen murmured, feeling a familiar surge of gratitude and love for the woman who had raised him single-handedly. As they stepped out of their modest home and into the chilly morning air, he couldn't help but wonder if there was someone out there who shared his same resilient spirit, and perhaps even his face, navigating life in a world so different from his own.

Chosen's fingers ached as he tightened the worn-out shoelaces of his secondhand sneakers. His breath formed misty clouds in the frosty air while he leaned against the graffiti-covered wall. With each passing car, he mentally calculated the odds of catching a ride to work. He couldn't afford to miss another shift.

"Hey, Chosen! Need a lift?" A voice called out. A beat-up pickup truck slowed down beside him and he recognized the driver as one of the neighbors from his apartment building.

"Thanks, Mr. Jenkins," Chosen replied with a grateful smile, hopping into the passenger seat. It was not much but it was these small acts of kindness that made the struggles of life in Brooksville bearable.

As the truck rumbled through potholed streets, Chosen glanced at the cracked rearview mirror and caught sight of his reflection. Dark circles marred the area under his eyes, a testament to his sleepless nights spent worrying about bills and job applications. Still, he held onto his determination with fierce tenacity.

"Kid, I don't know how you do it," Mr. Jenkins said, shaking his head as they pulled up to the factory where Chosen worked. "Always getting back up no matter how many times life knocks you down."

"Can't let life win, right?" Chosen responded, forcing a lighthearted tone. But deep down, he questioned how long he could keep pushing forward.

"Take care of yourself, Chosen," Mr. Jenkins warned before driving off, leaving Chosen standing outside the factory gates. The harsh clang of machinery echoed through the air as he steeled himself for another grueling shift.

Every break, every stolen moment between tasks, Chosen's thoughts drifted back to Greenfield—a place he had only ever visited in his imagination. He wondered what it would be like to live there, amidst the manicured lawns and white picket fences. A place where life did not feel like a constant battle.

"Chosen!" His supervisor barked, snapping him back to reality. "Get back to work!"

"Sorry, Sir," Chosen mumbled, refocusing on the task at hand. He couldn't afford to get lost in daydreams; he had a life to build for himself, despite the odds stacked against him.

As the day wore on, Chosen's body grew weary but his mind remained sharp. He found creative ways to speed up his tasks, earning approving nods from his coworkers. With each completed job, he felt his confidence grow—a stark contrast to the polished self-assurance that always seemed to come so naturally to Ted.

"Good work today, Chosen," his supervisor grudgingly praised as the shift finally came to an end. "Keep it up and we'll see about that promotion."

"Thank you, Sir," Chosen said, a flicker of hope igniting within him as he clocked out. He knew that even if he could never escape the gritty streets of Brooksville, he could still make something of himself. A small smile tugged at his lips as he made his way home, already planning how he would tackle tomorrow's challenges with the same resourcefulness and determination that had carried him this far.

Meanwhile, miles away in Greenfield, Ted was blissfully unaware of the daily struggles faced by the brother he had never met. But as fate would have it, their worlds were about to collide, and the stark differences between their upbringings would soon be brought to light.

The evening sun cast a warm, golden glow on the modest home that Chosen and Melissa shared, painting long shadows across the narrow street. Chosen's footsteps were light as he approached the front door, the anticipation of seeing his mother bringing a smile to his face. Despite the challenges they faced, the bond between them had only grown stronger over the years.

"Chosen!" Melissa exclaimed, her eyes lighting up as she opened the door. "You made it home earlier than I expected. How was work?"

"Long day but I managed," Chosen replied, stepping inside and kicking off his shoes. He glanced around the cozy living room, taking in the well-worn furniture and the faded family photos on the walls, each one a testament to their resilience.

"Sit down, honey, I'll make you some dinner," Melissa insisted, leading him toward the kitchen. As they sat at the small table, Chosen couldn't help but notice the worry lines etched across his mother's face. Though his heart ached for her, he knew that showing any sign of weakness would only make things harder.

"Mom, don't stress too much about the bills," Chosen said, trying to sound confident. "I'm working hard and things are going to get better."

Melissa sighed, looking into his eyes with a mix of gratitude and concern. "I know you are, sweetheart. I just wish life hadn't been so tough on you."

"Hey, I'm tougher than it," Chosen grinned, leaning back in his chair. As if on cue, his phone buzzed in his pocket and he pulled it out to see a text from Natalie.

"Everything okay?" Melissa asked, noticing the change in his expression.

"Yep, just Natalie checking in," Chosen replied, smiling as he read her words of encouragement. He would never admit it but her unwavering support had been his lifeline on more than one occasion. "I'm going to head out for a bit and see her."

"Give her my love," Melissa said, reaching across the table to squeeze his hand. "And be careful out there."

Chosen nodded, standing up and pulling his jacket on. As he exited the house, he felt a familiar surge of protectiveness toward his mother. He would do anything to shield her from the harsh realities of their world, even if it meant putting up a tough front.

The streets of Brooksville were darker now, bathed in the pale light of the streetlamps. Chosen's footsteps echoed as he made his way to Natalie's apartment, his thoughts filled with the stark contrast between his life and Ted's. But dwelling on what could have been would not change anything; all he could do was face each day with determination and hope.

"Chosen!" Natalie exclaimed as she opened her door, her red curls bouncing with excitement. "You came!"

"Of course I did," Chosen replied, stepping inside. "You're my rock, Nat. And I need that right now."

Natalie's eyes softened and she wrapped her arms around him in a tight hug. In her embrace, he allowed himself a rare moment of vulnerability, knowing that with her, he did not have to pretend to be unbreakable. Together, they faced the world and whatever challenges it threw their way.

The sun cast a warm golden glow over the Thompson household as Ted sat cross-legged on the plush carpet in his bedroom. He was rummaging through a dusty old box that had been hidden away in the attic, tucked beneath a pile of worn-out quilts. The musty smell of the box's contents filled his nostrils as he pulled out various items—faded photographs, newspaper clippings, and a stack of letters tied together with a fraying ribbon.

"David! Susan!" Ted called out, lifting the letters to his face, examining them closely. "What are these?"

His adoptive parents appeared in the doorway, exchanging glances before David spoke. "Those are letters from your birth mother, Melissa."

Ted's heart skipped a beat as he carefully untied the ribbon. His hands trembled slightly as he unfolded the first letter, dated just a few months after his adoption. The ink had smeared in places but the words were still legible, each one resonating deeply within him.

"Dear David and Susan," the letter began, "I hope this letter finds you well and that my dear boy is growing strong and healthy under your loving care. Not a day goes by when I don't think of him and Chosen, wondering how their lives have turned out…"

"Chosen?" Ted murmured, looking up at his adoptive parents. "Who's Chosen?"

"Your twin brother," Susan replied gently, her voice wavering. "We didn't know about him until much later."

"Does he…does he live with our birth mother?" Ted asked, his eyes scanning the rest of the letter as he awaited their response.

"Yes, they're in Brooksville," David confirmed, his hand resting on Susan's shoulder for support.

A sudden sense of longing welled up inside Ted, his curiosity piqued by the mention of his twin brother and birth mother. As much as he loved his life in Greenfield, a part of him yearned to explore his origins and connect with the family he never knew.

"Can I…can I meet them?" Ted asked hesitantly, glancing between his adoptive parents.

"Of course," Susan assured him, her eyes glistening with unshed tears. "We've always wanted you to have the opportunity to know your roots. But we also wanted you to be old enough to understand and make that decision for yourself."

"Thank you," Ted whispered, clutching the letters to his chest. He knew that, no matter what he discovered about his past, his love and gratitude for David and Susan would remain unwavering. They had given him a stable, loving home—something he would cherish for the rest of his days.

As he continued reading through Melissa's letters, each one filled with heartfelt emotion, Ted couldn't help but wonder how different his life could have been. Would he have the same polished and confident demeanor if he had grown up in Brooksville? Or would he be more like Chosen—resourceful, street-smart, and toughened by hardship?

"Whatever happens," Ted murmured to himself, imbued with a newfound determination, "I'll face it head-on, just like Chosen does. We may come from different worlds but we're still brothers."

Just as Ted was about to put the letter away, he caught a glimpse of an old photograph tucked between the pages. It was slightly worn and creased around the edges but the image was striking nonetheless. There, standing side by side, were Chosen and Melissa, their arms wrapped tightly around each other in a loving embrace.

Ted couldn't help but stare at the picture, his fingers tracing the outlines of their faces, noting the identical features that he shared with Chosen: the same short, dark hair, the athletic build, and the strong jawline. There was no denying that they were brothers, even if their lives had taken very different paths.

"Wow," he whispered, holding the photo closer to his face. "We could be twins." The thought sent a shiver down his spine. If not for a twist of fate, he might have been the one living in Brooksville, facing the challenges Chosen had faced his entire life.

"Ted?" Susan's voice interrupted his thoughts. "Are you all right?"

He looked up at her, the photograph still clutched in his hand. "Yeah, I'm fine. Just…thinking about how similar we look."

David nodded in agreement. "It's uncanny, isn't it? Sometimes I wonder if there would ever be any confusion or mistaken identity between the two of you."

"Maybe," Ted replied, his mind racing with possibilities. He envisioned what it would be like to walk down the streets of Brooksville, perhaps being greeted by people who mistook him for Chosen. Would they see the differences between them despite their outward similarities? And how would Chosen react to having an identical brother suddenly appear in his life?

"Ted," Susan said gently, placing a hand on his shoulder. "Remember that no matter what happens, you'll always have our support, and we'll always be here for you."

"Thank you," he murmured, his heart swelling with love for his adoptive parents. He knew that the journey ahead would be filled with uncertainty but he was determined to embrace the challenge and face it head-on.

As Ted stood in his childhood room, the photograph of Chosen and Melissa clutched tightly in his hand, he couldn't help but feel a sense of anticipation mixed with apprehension. He knew that meeting his brother and exploring their shared past would undoubtedly lead to clashes between their different upbringings and perspectives, but he also felt a strong desire to understand the life he might have led and to connect with the family he never knew.

"Are you ready for this?" He asked himself, taking a deep breath as he stared at the photograph one last time. With a resolute nod, Ted placed the picture back into the envelope, tucked it securely under his arm, and took the first step toward discovering his true identity.

Chapter 2

Ethan, Ted's childhood friend, had come for a visit to help sort through old photographs and trinkets. Little did they know that their lives would soon take an unexpected turn.

"Hey, Ted, what's this?" Ethan asked, holding up a dusty, yellowing envelope that he'd found wedged between two photo albums.

Ted furrowed his brow as he took the envelope from Ethan's hand. He noticed the name 'Melissa' written in elegant cursive on the front. His heart skipped a beat as he recognized the name of his birth mother. Carefully, he slid a finger under the flap, tearing it open to reveal a folded sheet of paper inside.

"Wow," he whispered, his eyes widening in surprise as he read the first few lines. "It's a letter from Melissa."

"Your birth mom?" Ethan's curiosity piqued as he leaned in closer to get a better look. "What does it say?"

Taking a deep breath, Ted began to read the letter aloud:

"Dear Ted,

I hope this letter finds you well. It has been years since I last saw you, and although we have never had the chance to connect, I want you to know that not a single day goes by without me thinking of you. You have always been in my heart, and I have always wished for your happiness and success."

As he continued reading, the words painted a picture of a life that could have been, one filled with love and warmth from a mother who had chosen to give him up, but never truly let him go. A pang of sadness and longing washed over Ted, leaving him feeling a sudden, urgent need to meet the woman who had brought him into this world.

"Ted, are you okay?" Ethan asked, placing a hand on his friend's shoulder sensing the turmoil within him.

"Yeah," Ted replied, swallowing hard as he blinked back tears. "I just…I can't believe it. She wrote to me all those years ago and I never knew."

"Maybe it's time you found out more about her," Ethan suggested gently, understanding the emotions that were bubbling beneath the surface. "You deserve to know your roots, man."

"Maybe you're right," Ted said, his voice wavering slightly. "I've always wondered about her but I never thought I'd actually have a chance to find her."

"Hey, we're a team, remember?" Ethan replied, giving Ted's shoulder a reassuring squeeze. "We'll figure this out together." The close bond between the two friends was evident in that moment, the trust and loyalty they had for each other shining through.

With determination setting in, Ted set the letter down on the table and looked at Ethan. "So what do you think? Do we try to find Melissa?"

Ethan leaned back in his chair, eyes focused on Ted as he considered the proposition. "Yeah, I think we should.

You've got a right to know who she is, and maybe she can help us understand your past better."

"Alright then," Ted said, taking a deep breath to steady himself. "Let's do it. But where do we even begin?"

"Let me see the letter again," Ethan requested, reaching for the worn paper. He scanned the contents, pausing at the return address in the top corner. "She lived in Brooksville when she wrote this. Maybe we could start there?"

"Brooksville…" Ted repeated, the name of the town feeling foreign on his lips. "Okay, it's as good a place to start as any."

As they began discussing their plans, an air of excitement enveloped them. This journey would take them into uncharted territory, delving into a past that Ted had long kept buried. Together, they would face the unknown, driven by the shared desire to uncover the truth about Ted's birth mother.

"Promise me something, Ethan," Ted said, his eyes reflecting the emotions swirling inside him. "No matter what we find out, we'll stick together, okay?"

"Of course," Ethan replied without hesitation, his loyalty unwavering. "We're in this together, all the way."

With that promise in place, they set to work, their determination to find Melissa fueling their every move. Little did they know, their journey would bring them face-to-face with more than they ever imagined.

The early morning sun cast long shadows on the pavement as Ted and Ethan loaded their bags into the trunk of Ted's sleek, black sedan. The excitement of their impending journey mingled with the crisp, cool air, leaving them feeling invigorated and alive. As they got into the car, the leather seats felt cold beneath them, but they knew that once the engine roared to life, the warmth would soon follow.

"Ready for this?" Ethan asked, his blue eyes shining with anticipation as he buckled his seatbelt.

"More than ever," Ted replied, his hands gripping the wheel. He took a deep breath, savoring the moment before they set off on their adventure.

As the engine hummed and the car pulled out onto the open road, they couldn't help but feel like explorers setting sail for uncharted territory. The world stretched out before them, filled with possibility and mystery. Ted's heart raced in time with the beat of the tires against the asphalt and he found himself grinning at the thought of what lay ahead.

"Brooksville, here we come," Ethan announced, adjusting the rearview mirror so he could watch the familiar landscape slipping away behind them. "You know, I've always wanted to go on a road trip like this. Just two friends, hitting the open road, chasing after a mystery."

"Me too," Ted admitted, keeping his eyes fixed on the horizon. "I just never expected it to be under these circumstances."

Hours passed as they drove, the scenery shifting from bustling city streets to the rolling hills and open fields of the countryside. Ted couldn't help but feel a growing sense of nervous anticipation the closer they drew to Brooksville. This was where his story had begun—a place he had no memory of, yet it had shaped so much of who he was.

As the afternoon sun dipped low in the sky, they arrived at a local gas station on the outskirts of Brooksville. Ted's hands trembled slightly as he pulled up to the pump, his heart pounding in his chest. This was it, the first real step toward uncovering the truth about his past.

"Hey," Ethan said softly, noticing the tension in Ted's posture. "You okay?"

Ted took a deep breath, trying to steady himself. "Yeah, I'm fine. Just…nervous, I guess."

"Understandable," Ethan replied, placing a reassuring hand on Ted's shoulder. "But we're in this together, remember? Whatever we find here, we'll face it head-on and deal with it as a team."

"Right," Ted agreed, forcing a smile. He climbed out of the car, his legs feeling unsteady beneath him, and began fueling up. The sound of gasoline flowing into the tank echoed in his ears, somehow amplifying the intensity of the moment.

As they stood there, the weight of their journey settling upon them, they couldn't help but feel a sense of foreboding. What would they find in Brooksville? And more importantly, were they truly prepared for the answers that awaited them? Only time would tell, but one thing was certain: they were in this together, for better or worse.

The sun dipped lower in the sky, casting an orange glow over the parked cars as Ted and Ethan stood by the gas pump, their anticipation a palpable force. An old pickup truck rumbled into the station and came to a halt near them. The door creaked open and out stepped a young man who was the mirror image of Ted.

Ted's breath caught in his throat as he stared at his doppelgänger. There, just a few feet away, stood Chosen, his long-lost twin brother. His heart raced as the shock and disbelief washed over him. It felt like time had stopped, leaving only the two of them standing in the fading twilight.

"Hey," Chosen said, squinting against the sun as he eyed Ted warily. "You look…familiar."

Ted swallowed hard, struggling to control the anger that threatened to boil over. "Yeah? Well, I should hope so. We're twins."

Chosen's eyes widened, his own surprise reflected in Ted's face. He took a step back, visibly shaken. "What are you talking about?"

"Melissa," Ted spat, his voice shaking with barely restrained fury. "Our birth mother. She kept you but she gave me up for adoption. And now I want to know why."

Chosen's brow furrowed as he tried to make sense of the situation. "I don't know what you're talking about, man. My mom never mentioned any of this. You must be mistaken."

"Am I?" Ted shot back, pulling the letter from his pocket and thrusting it into Chosen's hands. "This is her handwriting. She wrote this to my adoptive parents. I'm not making this up."

Chosen scanned the letter, his face pale, and then looked back up at Ted with pained eyes. He opened his mouth to speak but no words came out. Instead, he just stared at his newfound brother, the weight of the truth settling heavily upon him.

"Look," Chosen said finally, his voice barely audible. "I don't know what to tell you. I truly didn't know about any of this. But if it's true…if we really are brothers…" He hesitated, searching Ted's face for understanding. "Then maybe we can figure this out together."

Ted clenched his fists, trying to stem the tide of emotions that threatened to overwhelm him. His chest tightened as he struggled to reconcile the anger he felt toward Melissa with the unexpected bond he now shared with Chosen. It was a whirlwind of confusion, hurt, and longing—a storm of feelings he was ill-equipped to navigate.

"Fine," he bit out through gritted teeth, making an effort to rein in his frustration. "But I want answers, Chosen. And I won't stop until I get them."

The air between the two brothers grew increasingly thick with tension as their voices rose in volume and intensity. Ted felt a cold fire raging within him, fueled by resentment and unanswered questions. His fists tightened further at his sides as he stared down Chosen, who was mirroring his own defensive stance.

"Answers?" Chosen shot back, his voice laced with bitterness. "You think I have all the answers? I just found out you exist! You want to blame someone? Blame Melissa!"

Ted's eyes flashed with anger at the mention of their birth mother. "Oh, trust me," he snarled, "I have more than enough blame for her."

"Hey!" Ethan interjected, trying to defuse the situation. "Guys, maybe we should take a step back and calm down. We're not going to get anywhere like this."

"Stay out of it, Ethan!" Ted snapped, his gaze never leaving Chosen. "This is between me and him."

Chosen's face twisted into a grimace as he took a step closer to Ted, their chests nearly touching. "Fine, then let's talk about her," he spat. "You think she wanted to give you up? She had no choice!"

"Really?" Ted scoffed, the venom in his voice palpable. "Because from where I'm standing, it looks like she chose you over me. So don't lecture me about choices!"

Their heated exchange had caught the attention of those around them. The gas station attendant peered through the window from inside the shop, eyes wide with concern. A couple exiting the store paused, their curiosity piqued by the escalating argument. Even a man filling up his car couldn't help but glance over, drawn to the commotion.

"Look," Chosen said, his voice tight with emotion as he met Ted's glare with equal ferocity. "I don't know why she did what she did, but I do know that we're not going to figure it out by tearing each other apart."

Ted's jaw clenched as he processed Chosen's words. He wanted to lash out, to let his rage carry him away like a tidal wave. But beneath the anger, there was something else—a flicker of hope, a yearning for understanding that refused to be extinguished.

"Fine," Ted muttered through gritted teeth, his voice strained and raw. "But we're in this together now. And if you're lying to me…if you're hiding anything from me…" His eyes locked onto Chosen's once more, the fury still simmering just below the surface. "You'll regret it."

Chosen nodded stiffly, the unspoken agreement hanging heavy in the air between them. They had reached an uneasy truce but the road ahead was far from certain, and the shadows of their shared past loomed large over their newfound connection.

Ethan, who had been watching the heated exchange between Ted and Chosen with growing concern, finally stepped forward, placing a hand on Ted's shoulder. "Hey, man," he said softly, his voice steady despite the tension in the air. "Let's take a step back, alright? We're not going to get anywhere like this."

Ted's breathing was ragged, his chest heaving as he tried to regain control of himself. He could feel the weight of Ethan's hand anchoring him, a reminder of their long-standing friendship and shared history. It was enough to keep the fire within him from consuming everything.

"Right," Ted muttered, nodding stiffly. He broke eye contact with Chosen, turning instead to face Ethan. "Let's go."

"Good call," Ethan agreed, giving Ted's shoulder a reassuring squeeze before releasing it. Together, they began to walk away from the confrontation, leaving a bewildered Chosen standing in front of the gas station.

As they climbed into Ted's car, Ted couldn't help but wonder what would have happened if Ethan had not intervened. Would he have lost himself completely to his anger, lashing out at the twin brother he had only just discovered?

His heart raced with equal parts gratitude and fear—gratitude for the steadying presence of his friend, and fear of the darkness that seemed to be lurking just beneath the surface, waiting for a chance to break free.

The car's tires crunched over gravel as they pulled out of the gas station, escaping the curious gazes of the attendant and other customers. The sky above them had grown darker, heavy clouds threatening rain and mirroring the tempestuous emotions brewing inside Ted.

The windshield wipers battled against the pouring rain, their rhythmic swishing a sharp contrast to the heavy silence that hung between Ted and Ethan. The tension inside the car was palpable.

"Man, I didn't expect that," Ethan said finally, breaking the silence as he glanced over at Ted. "I mean, running into your twin brother like that…"

Ted swallowed hard, feeling a lump forming in his throat. "Neither did I. And just when we're trying to find Melissa… It's like fate has a twisted sense of humor."

"Maybe it's a sign," Ethan suggested, trying to lighten the mood. "Maybe it means we're getting closer to finding her."

"Or maybe it's a warning," Ted countered, his voice cracking slightly. "A warning that this whole journey is a bad idea."

"Hey, don't say that," Ethan chided gently. "We've come this far and we're not stopping now. We'll find Melissa and you'll get the answers you deserve."

"But what if those answers only lead to more pain?" Ted asked, his eyes glistening with unshed tears. "What if confronting her only makes things worse?"

"Then we'll face it together," Ethan replied firmly, giving Ted a determined look. "Like we always do."

Ted sighed, allowing himself a small smile. "Thanks, Ethan. I don't know what I'd do without you."

"Probably get into a lot more fights," Ethan joked, grinning back at him. "But seriously, man, I'm here for you. Always have been, always will be."

As they continued driving through the rain-soaked streets, Ted couldn't help but think about his newfound sibling. The anger he had felt toward Chosen was still simmering beneath the surface, but now it was mingled with something else—a sense of longing for a connection he had never known he was missing.

"Maybe after we find Melissa…I could try talking to him again," Ted mused, staring out into the dark night. "You know, without all the anger and resentment."

"Sounds like a plan," Ethan agreed, nodding approvingly. "But first things first. Let's find your birth mother and get some answers."

Ted nodded, his resolve strengthening. They would find Melissa, no matter what obstacles stood in their way. And maybe, just maybe, along the way, he'd be able to forge a bond with the brother he never knew he had.

"Let's do this," he whispered, his voice full of determination as they drove on into the night.

Chapter 3

After a bit of driving, Ted noticed that Chosen's truck was in the rearview mirror following them. Chosen then drove up alongside Ted as they were both driving and began to motion for Ted to roll down the window. Once opened, Chosen said, "follow me," then sped ahead. Not even a quarter mile further, Chosen signaled as he approached and made a left turn and Ted followed him into what appeared to be an narrow alley.

The narrow alley was cloaked in shadows, its dim light emanating from a single flickering streetlamp above. The cold air hung heavy with the stench of damp earth and rotting garbage, a fitting atmosphere for the intense confrontation that was about to unfold.

Puddles littered the cracked pavement, reflecting the feeble light and distorting it into twisted shapes. The walls on either side seemed to close in, as if they were watching the scene play out with bated breath.

Both vehicles stopped. First, Chosen exited his truck. Then, while Ethan remained in the car, Ted hopped out and stood there, his heart pounding furiously in his chest, and his hands clenched into fists at his sides. His breathing came in ragged gasps as he struggled to make sense of the maelstrom of emotions swirling within him. Rage and abandonment coursed through his veins, fueled by the resentment he harbored toward Chosen and Melissa.

He had spent years believing that they didn't want him, that they had cast him aside like a piece of trash, leaving a gaping hole in his soul that no amount of love from his adoptive family could fill.

"Chosen," Ted spat as he approached him, the name tasting bitter on his tongue. "How could you just forget about me?"

"Ted, it wasn't like that," Chosen replied, his voice laced with regret. "We were just kids. We didn't have a choice."

As Ted looked into his brother's dark eyes, so much like his own, he saw the genuine remorse there. But it did little to quell the storm raging inside him. It wasn't just Chosen; it was their mother, Melissa, who had broken his heart time and time again. The woman who had given birth to them, yet chose to keep only one son by her side.

"Ted, you don't understand," Chosen continued, his voice barely more than a whisper. "She's struggled with guilt every day since she gave you up. It destroyed her."

"Destroyed her?" Ted scoffed, his anger boiling over. "What about me? What about the pain I've had to endure? The nights I spent wondering why I wasn't good enough for my own mother?"

As the full weight of his emotions threatened to crush him, Ted felt something snap inside him. He could no longer contain the fury and bitterness that had festered within him for far too long. All he could see was the brother who got to keep their mother's love, while he was left with nothing but a gaping void in his heart.

"Chosen," he whispered, his voice trembling with barely suppressed rage. "I'll never forgive you for this. You took everything from me."

"Enough!" Chosen yelled, his face a mixture of anger and frustration. "I didn't choose this life for you, Ted. I didn't abandon you. But I'm not going to stand here and let you blame me for everything that's gone wrong in your life."

Ted clenched his fists, feeling the cold air biting at his skin while the searing heat of rage burned inside him. His eyes darted around the alley, landing on a stray brick lying just a few feet away, its sharp edges illuminated by the faint glow of a flickering streetlamp. The brick seemed to beckon him, a desperate solution to end this unbearable pain.

"Chosen, you're nothing but a reminder of what I didn't have," Ted spat out, his voice shaking with anger. "You're the one who got to stay with her, while I was left to rot in that godforsaken orphanage!"

"Ted, please," Chosen pleaded, taking a step closer, his hands raised in a gesture of surrender. "I want to help you. Let's talk this out."

But Ted could no longer hear his brother's words. He saw only the ghost of a mother he'd never known and the brother who had stolen her love. In a blind fury, Ted lunged toward the brick, grabbing it with both hands, feeling its chilling weight grounding him in a terrible purpose.

"Stay back!" Ted screamed, his breath fogging in the icy air as he brandished the brick like a weapon. "I swear, I'll do it!"

"Ted, don't!" Chosen cried, his voice strained with panic.

In a split second, all of Ted's pent-up rage and resentment erupted, propelling him forward. With a guttural scream, he swung the brick at Chosen, striking him on the side of the head.

The sickening crack echoed through the alley, amplifying Ted's sudden realization of the horror he had just unleashed. Chosen crumpled to the ground, blood pooling around his still form.

"Chosen!" Ted gasped, dropping the brick as if it burned him. He stared down at his brother's lifeless body, his own hands now stained with the thick crimson evidence of his violent act. "No, no, no…What have I done?"

Ted's heart hammered in his chest, threatening to burst from the weight of the devastating truth: he had just killed his own brother. Panic clawed at his mind, forcing him to confront the consequences he would face if he turned himself in. His adoptive family, the only ones who had ever truly loved him, would be shattered by his actions. And for what? The release of a lifetime's worth of pain and jealousy?

As Ted stood there, trembling with shock and terror, he knew that one fateful decision had changed everything. The life he had known was gone, and the path before him was darker and more treacherous than the dimly lit alley that had become the stage for his unforgivable crime.

Ted's breath caught in his throat as he stared at Chosen's lifeless body. The blood on his hands seemed to sear into his skin, branding him with the guilt of fratricide.

He took a shaky step back, his mind racing with desperation.

"Think, Ted...think!" He whispered hoarsely, forcing himself to focus on what needed to be done. He couldn't let this destroy everything he held dear; his adoptive family, their love and support, all of it would crumble if the world found out what he had done.

"Chosen, I'm so sorry," he choked out, swallowing hard against the lump in his throat. "But I have to do this."

His heart pounding, Ted grabbed Chosen's limp wrist and began to drag him further into the alley, wincing at the trail of blood that followed. He knew he had to hide the body, erase any connection to his crime, but where? Time was running out.

"Damn it, there has to be somewhere..." Ted muttered under his breath, scanning the shadowy recesses of the alley. His eyes fell upon a rusted dumpster, its lid partially ajar, and an idea formed in his panicked mind.

"Okay, okay, this might work," he whispered, pulling Chosen's body toward the dumpster. With a grunt, he heaved the limp form up and over the edge, wincing as it landed with a sickening thud among the trash within.

"God, forgive me," Ted prayed, wiping sweat from his brow. He turned his attention to the bloody trail, knowing he had to clean it up before anyone discovered the scene.

Rummaging through the nearby garbage, Ted found a tattered piece of cardboard. Biting his lip, he used it to scrape away the blood, doing his best to remove all traces of the violent confrontation. He worked with feverish determination, every second feeling like an eternity.

Please, let this be enough, he thought, his hands shaking as he scrubbed at the stubborn stains. The fear of losing everything he held dear threatened to consume him, but he pushed it down, focusing on the task at hand.

Finally, the alley's cobblestones were free of Chosen's blood and any incriminating evidence had been wiped away. Ted knew that he was far from safe, that the guilt and the constant threat of discovery would follow him like a shadow. But for now, he had done all he could to protect himself and his family.

"Goodbye, brother," he whispered, casting one last anguished look at the dumpster before stumbling out of the alley, his heart heavy with the burden of his actions and the secrets he now had to keep.

Ted stumbled out of the alley, his heart pounding like a jackhammer in his chest. The cold night air stung his lungs as he sucked in desperate breaths, trying to quell the rising tide of panic threatening to engulf him. He had taken a life—his own brother's life—and the enormity of what he had done bore down on him like a crushing weight.

"God, what have I done?" He whispered, his voice barely audible over the distant hum of city traffic. "How could I let things go this far?"

He leaned heavily against the side of a nearby building, feeling sick with guilt and fear. Images of Chosen's lifeless body filled his mind and Ted clenched his eyes shut, willing them away. But they remained, haunting him like specters from some terrible nightmare.

"Get a grip, Ted," he muttered under his breath, forcing himself to focus on the task at hand. The more time he spent wallowing in guilt, the greater the risk of someone discovering what he had done. "You need to think."

His thoughts raced in frantic circles, weighing the potential consequences of his actions. If he turned himself in, he would surely be sent to prison, leaving his adoptive parents heartbroken and shamed. Their love and support had been the bedrock of his life and he couldn't bear the thought of losing them.

"Is it worth it?" He whispered, his voice shaking. "Can I live with the guilt of covering up a crime?"

But the alternative—the risk of getting caught—seemed equally unbearable. His entire future hung in the balance, teetering precariously between two equally devastating outcomes.

"Ted, is that you?" A familiar voice called out, making him jump. He turned to see Ethan approaching, concern etched on his face. "What happened? You look like you've seen a ghost."

"Nothing…it's nothing," Ted stammered, struggling to maintain his composure. "Just a bit shaken up, is all."

"Are you sure?" Ethan asked, unconvinced. "You can talk to me, man. Something's clearly wrong."

Ted hesitated, torn between the need to confide in someone and the fear of revealing his terrible secret. Every fiber of his being screamed at him to tell the truth, but he knew that doing so would only put his friend in danger.

"Really, I'm fine," he insisted, forcing a brittle smile onto his face. "I just…I need some time alone right now, okay?"

Ethan studied him for a moment, his brow furrowed with worry. But eventually, he nodded, clapping Ted on the shoulder.

"Alright, man," he said softly. "But if you ever need someone to talk to, you know where to find me."

"Thanks, Ethan," Ted replied, his voice thick with unshed tears. He watched as his friend walked back to the car, leaving him alone with his guilt and his fears.

As the distance between them grew, Ted felt the weight of his actions settling heavily on his shoulders. He had made his choice, and now he was trapped—caught between the crushing guilt of what he had done and the constant terror of discovery.

And in that dark, cold, rainy night, Ted realized that no matter what the future held, he would never truly escape the consequences of his actions.

Ted's heart raced as he stood in the dimly lit alley, his eyes darting back and forth, searching for a better yet suitable hiding place for Chosen's lifeless body. The cold night air bit at his exposed skin but it paled in comparison to the chill that ran down his spine as he considered the consequences of his actions.

"Come on, come on," he muttered under his breath, his desperation growing with each passing second. He knew he needed to act quickly, lest someone discover him in this compromising position. His gaze finally settled on a large, industrial dumpster tucked into a shadowy corner that was much more obscured than where Chosen's body is now.

"Perfect," he whispered, his voice barely audible against the low hum of the city. Ted got in the dumpster and crouched down beside Chosen, his hands trembling as he wrapped them around the young man's limp form. With a grunt of effort, he hoisted the body onto his shoulder, staggering slightly under the weight before laying his body over the edge while he exited.

"Sorry, Chosen," Ted murmured, taking one last look at the face. Steeling himself, he picked him up, half-walked, half-stumbled toward the larger industrial dumpster, his every movement fueled by a desperate need to preserve what little was left of his old life.

As he reached the dumpster, Ted carefully lowered Chosen's body into the shadows, taking care to arrange it in such a way that it wouldn't be easily discovered. He took a deep, shuddering breath, trying to quell the rising sense of panic that threatened to consume him.

"Keep it together, Ted," he told himself, wiping his forehead with the back of his hand. "You can do this."

With Chosen's body hidden away, Ted turned his attention again to the scene of the crime to make sure he did not miss anything. He retrieved the stray brick he had used to strike Chosen, wincing as he noticed the dark stains that marred its surface. He tucked it into a nearby pile of debris, hoping that it would go unnoticed.

Please, please let this be enough, he thought, his heart hammering in his chest as he scanned the area for any other traces of his presence. He wiped away a few errant drops of blood with the sleeve of his jacket, grimacing at the cold, wet sensation against his skin.

Suddenly, he heard footsteps approaching, faint, but unmistakable in the stillness of the night. His pulse quickened and he ducked behind the dumpster, praying that he wouldn't be seen.

"Who's there?" A wary voice called out, causing Ted's breath to catch in his throat. He stayed as still as possible, hardly daring to breathe, his mind racing with potential excuses for his presence in the alley.

"Probably just a cat or something," the voice muttered after a moment and the footsteps continued on their way. Ted let out a shaky exhale, his heart pounding like a drum in his ears.

Too close, he thought, wiping sweat from his brow. *Way too close.*

Gathering the last of his resolve, Ted finished erasing any remaining evidence of the altercation and stepped out from behind the dumpster. He cast one final, anxious glance around the alley before hurrying away, the weight of his actions heavy on his shoulders and the fear of being caught gnawing at him relentlessly.

Ted's heart threatened to burst from his chest as he stumbled down the dimly lit street toward his car, the chilling wind biting at his exposed skin. His breaths came in ragged gasps, fogging up the air in front of him. With every step, the weight of what he'd done bore down on him, threatening to crush him under its enormity.

"God, what have I done?" Ted muttered to himself, his voice barely audible over the howling wind. The image of Chosen's lifeless body, hidden away in that dark alley, haunted him.

"Hey, man, are you okay?" A passerby asked, concern etched across his face. Ted flinched, his head snapping toward the stranger. He hadn't realized how lost he was in his own thoughts.

"Y-yeah, I'm fine," Ted stammered, struggling to put on a brave face. "Just a little…shaken up, is all."

"Alright, well, take care of yourself," the stranger said, giving him a reassuring pat on the shoulder before walking away. Ted forced a weak smile, the guilt gnawing at him like a ravenous beast.

As he continued down the street, Ted's thoughts raced, a whirlwind of emotions and fears. *Can I live with this? Can I really go on knowing I took someone's life? But if I turn myself in, it'll destroy everything I've built with my adoptive family. David, Susan…they don't deserve this.*

He clenched his fists, anger and determination flaring within him. "No, I can't let them suffer for my actions. I have to protect them, no matter what."

His resolve hardened, Ted began planning his next steps. "I need to figure out what to do. How can I keep them safe? What if the police find out? I've got to be careful, thorough."

"Hey, Ted! Where have you been?" Ethan called out, suddenly appearing from around a corner.

"Uh, I just needed some air," Ted lied, forcing a smile onto his face. "Had to clear my head, y'know?"

"Sure thing, man. Just don't go disappearing like that, okay?" Ethan said, slinging an arm around Ted's shoulders as they walked together toward their car.

"Promise," Ted murmured, the weight of his secret bearing down on him like a thousand tons. He knew he had to keep it buried deep inside, for the sake of those he loved. Even if it meant living with the guilt and fear, forever gnawing away at his soul.

Satisfied that he had done all he could, he stepped out of the alley, glancing over his shoulder one last time.

As he walked away, the weight of what he had done began to settle on his shoulders. His chest tightened with each step and he found it increasingly difficult to breathe. The guilt gnawed at him like a relentless hunger, leaving him feeling hollow and numb.

His thoughts raced, a chaotic whirlwind of fear and uncertainty. What if someone had seen him? What if they recognized him? The consequences of his actions loomed large in his mind, casting a dark shadow over his future. Should he confide in Ethan, he wondered. It seemed to him like his best option. Together they could figure out what to do next. After driving away from the alley, Ted shares what really just happened with Ethan and together they decide on what to do next: enlist help.

Ted's heart raced as he and Ethan walked down the dimly lit hallway of a rundown office building. The worn carpet beneath their feet seemed to soak up every ounce of hope they had left in them. Their desperation hung heavy in the air, like the stale odor of cigarette smoke that clung to the walls.

"Are you sure about this guy?" Ted asked, his voice trembling with anxiety.

"Positive," Ethan replied, trying to sound more confident than he felt. "My uncle said he's the best when it comes to shady situations."

As they reached the door marked 'Frank Douglas, Private Investigator', Ted hesitated for a moment before raising his hand to knock. His knuckles rapped against the worn wood, which echoed down the hallway.

"Come in," came the gruff voice from inside.

Ted opened the door and stepped into the office, Ethan following close behind. The room was dimly lit, with sunlight filtering through the grimy window blinds. Frank Douglas sat behind an old wooden desk, a half-empty bottle of whiskey and a stained coffee mug beside him. He was a man of average height, with broad shoulders that seemed to carry the weight of the world.

His face was rugged, bearing deep frown lines, and his unkempt salt-and-pepper hair framed his piercing gray eyes. A thin cigar hung limply from the corner of his mouth, its smoke swirling around him like a protective shroud.

"Have a seat, boys," he said gruffly, gesturing to the mismatched chairs opposite his desk. His voice bore the roughness of years of hard living and dangerous dealings.

Ted and Ethan exchanged a nervous glance before sinking into the creaky chairs. Ted's hands were clammy, gripping the edge of his seat, while Ethan's leg bounced anxiously. It was clear they were out of their element, and Frank could sense their desperation.

"Mr. Douglas," Ted began, his voice cracking under the pressure. "We…we need your help."

"Obviously," Frank replied, taking a swig from his whiskey bottle. "People don't come to me for sunshine and rainbows."

Ted swallowed hard, trying to find the courage to continue. "It's about a murder."

"Go on," Frank said, leaning back in his chair and studying the two young men before him.

Ethan chimed in, his voice barely louder than a whisper. "We need someone like you, someone who knows how to deal with this kind of thing."

Frank took another drag from his cigar, blowing out a thick plume of smoke as he considered their words. He could see the fear etched into their faces—the way Ted's eyes darted around, searching for any sign of danger, and the sweat that beaded on Ethan's brow. Their desperation was palpable, and Frank knew that they had nowhere else to turn.

"Alright," he finally said, stubbing out his cigar in the overflowing ashtray. "Tell me everything."

Ted's hands trembled as he recounted the chilling events that had led them to Frank's doorstep. The flickering neon sign outside cast eerie shadows across the room, amplifying the tension that filled the air. Ethan fidgeted nervously in his seat, occasionally chiming in with details that Ted had left out or forgotten.

"Sounds like you boys are in a real mess," Frank said, his gravelly voice cutting through the heavy silence. He leaned forward, resting his elbows on the cluttered desk and steepling his fingers. "You understand the risks involved in coming to me for help, right? There's no going back once we start down this path."

"We know," Ethan replied, his jaw clenched in determination. "We don't have any other choice."

Frank sighed, taking another swig of whiskey before setting the bottle down with a thud. "Alright, let's get one thing straight; I'm not in the business of playing hero. But I can help you dispose of Chosen's body and cover your tracks, if that's what you want."

Ted exchanged a hesitant glance with Ethan, who gave a barely perceptible nod. "Yes," Ted said, his voice barely audible. "We need to make sure there's no evidence connecting us to this…to Chosen's death."

"Good," Frank grunted, reaching into a drawer, and pulling out a crumpled map. He spread it out on the desk, tracing his finger along the lines of streets and alleys as he spoke. "First, we'll need to find a secure location, someplace isolated where no one will stumble across the body. Then, we'll need supplies: gloves, plastic sheeting, bleach, a hacksaw…You get the idea."

Ted's stomach churned at the thought of what they were about to do but he forced himself to focus on Frank's instructions. He had to be strong for his family and for himself.

"Once we've got everything in place," Frank continued, "I'll guide you through the process step by step. We'll make sure the body is unrecognizable and dispose of it in a way that leaves no trace. Then, we'll clean the area thoroughly, removing any evidence that could link you to the crime. It won't be easy, and it certainly won't be pleasant, but if you follow my directions exactly, you should be able to walk away from this nightmare with your lives intact."

"Thank you," Ted murmured, his heart pounding in his chest as the gravity of their situation sank in. They were about to cross a line that could never be uncrossed, and there was no telling what the consequences might be.

But for now, they had no choice but to trust Frank, and each other, if they wanted any chance of surviving the nightmare that had become their reality. Ted and Ethan first went to get the needed items from a nearby 24-hr store. It was still dark, so they then took Frank back to the alley to retrieve Chosen's lifeless body before heading to an secluded abandoned warehouse.

The abandoned warehouse loomed before them, its crumbling brick walls and shattered windows casting eerie shadows in the moonlight. The once bustling building now stood silent and desolate, swallowed by the darkness that clung to it like a shroud. The distant sound of a train whistle pierced the night air, a mournful reminder of the life that had long since abandoned this forsaken place.

"Here we are," Frank muttered as he led Ted and Ethan inside, his flashlight cutting through the darkness to reveal a vast, empty space littered with debris and the remnants of a bygone era. "This should be secluded enough for our purposes."

Ted's heart raced and he could feel the sweat pooling at the small of his back. He swallowed hard, trying to push down the bile rising in his throat. *Stay focused*, he thought.

"Alright," Frank said, his voice business-like as he began outlining the plan. "First, we'll lay out the plastic sheeting on the ground. That'll help contain any…mess, and make cleanup easier. Ethan, start unrolling it over there."

Ethan nodded, his face pale but determined as he set to work. Ted watched him for a moment, feeling a strange mix of gratitude and guilt toward his friend. They were in this together, bound by loyalty and fear. But would their friendship survive the horrors they were about to commit?

"Next," Frank continued, addressing Ted, "you'll need to put on the gloves. Make sure they're tight, we can't afford any slips or fingerprints."

"Got it," Ted replied, his voice barely above a whisper as he pulled the latex gloves over his trembling hands.

"Once you've got the body on the plastic, we'll begin dismembering it. I know it sounds brutal but it's necessary if we want to make it unrecognizable. You'll need to use the hacksaw and work methodically, cutting through the joints first, then breaking down the larger pieces." Frank's voice was cold, detached, as if he were discussing a mundane task rather than the desecration of a human body.

"Okay," Ted said, his stomach churning at the thought of the grisly work ahead. He glanced over at Ethan, who was finishing up with the plastic sheeting, and saw his own fear reflected in his friend's eyes. They shared a look of grim determination, silently acknowledging the pact they had made: they would see this through, no matter what it took.

As they carefully placed Chosen's lifeless form on the plastic, Ted felt a wave of nausea wash over him. He tried to focus on Frank's instructions but the enormity of what they were doing threatened to overwhelm him. This was wrong, so horribly wrong, but there was no turning back now.

"Remember," Frank warned, his voice low and urgent, "precision is key. Don't rush and be thorough. The last thing we need is a stray hair or a drop of blood giving us away."

Ted nodded, his throat tight with the effort of holding back tears. As he picked up the hacksaw, the weight of their actions bore down on him, suffocating and inescapable. But for his parents, for Ethan, he would do whatever it took. And so, with a heavy heart and trembling hands, he began the gruesome task that lay before them.

Ted's hands shook as he gripped the handle of the hacksaw, its serrated edge glinting menacingly in the dim light. He swallowed hard, trying to steady himself as Ethan pulled on a pair of latex gloves, an odd sense of detachment settling over him.

"Alright," Frank said, his tone matter-of-fact. "First, you need to make an incision down the center of the chest, from the collarbone to the abdomen."

Ted hesitated for a moment, his heart pounding in his ears. He glanced at Ethan, who gave a tight nod of encouragement. Taking a deep breath, Ted pressed the blade against Chosen's cold skin and began to saw.

"Good, good," Frank muttered, watching closely. "Now, separate the ribs from the sternum."

Ethan stepped in, wielding a pair of heavy-duty shears with surprising precision. Sweat beaded on his forehead as he cut through bone and cartilage, the grisly snapping sound echoing through the warehouse.

"Jesus Christ," Ted whispered before hurling, his stomach roiling. "How did we get here?"

"Keep going," Frank urged, his eyes darting between the two young men. "We don't have much time."

Ted forced himself to focus, pushing away the sick feeling that threatened to consume him. He couldn't afford to fall apart now, not when so much was at stake. As he continued to work alongside Ethan, their movements synchronized by necessity, he could feel the tension building between them like an electric charge.

"Cut the limbs at the joints," Frank instructed, pointing to the elbow and knee. "It'll be easier to dispose of that way."

"Is this really necessary?" Ted asked, struggling to keep his voice steady. The thought of dismembering Chosen sent a fresh wave of panic through him, but he knew they had to follow Frank's instructions to the letter.

"Trust me," Frank replied, his gaze unwavering. "It's the only way to ensure that nothing can be traced back to you."

Ted tried not to think about the fact that they were mutilating the body of someone they knew, his identical twin brother. But, because they were identical, in Ted's mind it began to feel as though he was doing everything to himself. He tried to continue and focused on the task at hand, cutting through muscle and tendon with a grim determination born of desperation.

"Almost there," Ethan said, his voice strained as he severed the last limb. He looked up at Ted, his blue eyes clouded with fear and exhaustion. "We're going to get through this, alright?"

"Right," Ted whispered, setting down the hacksaw and wiping his bloodied hands on his jeans. "We have to."

As they wrapped Chosen's dismembered remains in plastic sheeting, Ted couldn't help but feel a profound sense of dread settling over him like a heavy shroud. They had done what needed to be done but at what cost? Would they ever truly be free of the horrors they had witnessed, and committed, in this dark, forsaken place?

With Chosen's remains wrapped and hidden, Ted couldn't shake the feeling that they were being watched. The warehouse seemed to breathe with a sinister energy, as though it, too, had become an accomplice in their crime. He forced himself to focus on what came next.

"Alright," Ethan said, his voice shaking slightly as he followed Frank's instructions. "Now we've got to clean up. We can't leave any trace of ourselves or Chosen here."

Ted's mind raced with the images of the gruesome task they had just completed. He tried to suppress the rising bile in his throat, steeling himself for the work ahead. He couldn't afford to break down now. As much as he wanted to escape this nightmare, there was still more to do.

"Right, let's start with the floor," Ted suggested, his voice barely audible. "We'll need to scrub every inch to make sure there's no blood or tissue left behind."

"Got it," Ethan replied, grabbing a bucket and filling it with water and bleach, as per Frank's advice. They worked in silence, each lost in their own thoughts as they methodically wiped away the evidence of their actions.

As Ted scrubbed, his mind swirled with guilt and fear. What if someone found out? What if they made a mistake in covering their tracks? His heart hammered in his chest and he fought to keep his breathing steady.

"Hey," Ethan said softly, noticing Ted's distress. "We're doing everything we can to make sure we don't get caught. Trust me, we'll be okay."

"Will we, Ethan?" Ted whispered, pausing to look at his friend. "How can we ever be okay after this?"

Ethan hesitated, his eyes searching for some reassuring words, but he remained silent. It was a question neither of them could answer.

"Let's just focus on getting this done," Ted sighed, returning to his task.

As they moved methodically through the warehouse, carefully wiping down surfaces and disposing of anything that could implicate them, Ted couldn't help but feel a strange sense of detachment. His body seemed to be acting on autopilot, following Ethan's instructions without question while his mind swam with dark thoughts.

"Ted," Ethan said, snapping him back to reality. "We're almost finished. Just need to double-check everything."

"Right," Ted muttered, forcing himself to concentrate on their surroundings, searching for any overlooked detail.

Finally, after hours of painstaking work, they stood in the center of the warehouse. Gone were the traces of blood and gore, replaced by a sterile emptiness that somehow felt even more chilling.

"Is it enough?" Ted asked quietly, his voice barely audible above the distant hum of the train tracks outside.

"It has to be," Ethan replied grimly. "We've done everything we can. Now we just have to live with it."

The warehouse's shadows seemed to recoil as Ted and Ethan rolled the tightly wrapped body of Chosen into a heavy-duty plastic barrel. Both men were drenched in sweat, their breathing labored from the physical exertion and the emotional turmoil that weighed heavily upon them.

"Almost there," Ethan said, his voice strained but resolute. He secured the lid on the barrel before wiping his brow with the back of his hand.

Ted nodded, taking a deep breath as they both stared at the container that held the secret they desperately needed to keep hidden. The guilt gnawed at him but he couldn't let it consume him now. They had to finish this.

"Help me move it," Ted said, grabbing one side of the barrel while Ethan took the other. Together, they maneuvered it toward the back of the warehouse, where a hidden trapdoor lay waiting.

"Once we drop it down there, it's done," Ethan murmured, his eyes meeting Ted's for a moment. "No going back."

"I know," Ted replied, swallowing hard. Their hands trembled slightly as they lifted the heavy barrel and carefully positioned it over the opening.

"Ready?" Ethan asked, his voice barely above a whisper.

"Ready," Ted confirmed, his heart pounding in his chest.

With one final push, they tipped the barrel over the edge, listening as it disappeared into the darkness below. The sound of it hitting the bottom echoed through the warehouse like a final farewell.

Chosen… I'm so sorry, Ted thought, his eyes welling up with tears that he refused to let fall.

"We did it," Ethan breathed out, relief washing over his face. "We protected ourselves."

"Did we, though?" Ted's mind raced with doubts. "What if someone finds out? What if we missed something?"

"Hey," Ethan said, grabbing Ted's shoulder and giving it a reassuring squeeze. "We'll stick together, alright? We'll keep each other in check and make sure this never comes back to haunt us."

"Right," Ted agreed, trying to quell the unease that squirmed in the pit of his stomach.

As they left the warehouse, the night air felt colder than before. Ted couldn't shake the feeling that this was only the beginning—a dark path they'd embarked on, with unknown dangers lurking around every corner.

"Stay strong," he told himself, gripping Ethan's arm for support. "Together, we can face whatever comes next."

Chapter 4

The afternoon sun cast long shadows over the quiet streets of Brooksville as Detective Mitchell steered the unmarked police car to a stop in front of Melissa Matthews' home. He glanced at Officer Johnson, who sat in the passenger seat, her eyes scanning the environment with keen interest.

"Looks like we're here," he muttered, unbuckling his seatbelt and opening the car door.

Officer Johnson followed suit, stepping out onto the cracked pavement. The air was thick with the scent of decay, and she could hear the distant hum of insects buzzing around the overgrown yard. They approached the house, taking in the dilapidated condition it was in. The once-white paint on the wooden exterior had peeled away, leaving behind a mottled pattern of grays and browns.

Broken windows were haphazardly patched with duct tape and cardboard, while tangled weeds and vines seemed to be the only things holding the sagging fence together.

Detective Mitchell sighed, feeling a familiar wave of frustration wash over him. *Another case, another rundown home*, he thought, rubbing his temples for a moment before refocusing on the task at hand.

"Stay sharp, Johnson," he instructed, as they made their way up the creaky steps to the front door.

Officer Johnson nodded, her gaze never leaving the house. She couldn't help but think about Chosen, the young man at the center of their investigation, and wondered how he had managed to thrive in such an environment. "There has to be more to this story," she mused, her determination to find answers fueling her every step.

As they reached the front door, they could see that it was just as neglected as the rest of the property. The doorknob was tarnished and loose, while the wood itself had warped over time, making it difficult to close properly. Detective Mitchell raised his hand to knock, and the door creaked ominously, as if it were protesting the disturbance.

"Let's see what Melissa has to say," he said quietly, his stern expression leaving no doubt about his commitment to uncovering the truth behind Chosen's disappearance.

"Right behind you, Detective," Officer Johnson replied, her own resolve unwavering as they waited for Melissa to answer the door.

Detective Mitchell's eyes narrowed as he approached the front door, the lines on his forehead deepening. Despite the heavy weight of the investigation resting on his shoulders, he maintained an air of authority that was only matched by his unyielding determination to uncover the truth. Beside him, Officer Johnson kept her posture relaxed, her friendly demeanor a deliberate contrast meant to ease potential tensions with Melissa.

"Ready?" Detective Mitchell asked in a low voice, glancing at Officer Johnson before rapping his knuckles against the weathered wood.

"Absolutely," she replied, offering a reassuring smile.

The faint sound of shuffling could be heard from within the house, followed by the creaking of floorboards as Melissa made her way to the door. When it finally swung open, Detective Mitchell and Officer Johnson were greeted by a woman who looked as though she had aged well beyond her years. Her shoulder-length wavy brown hair hung limp, framing a face worn down by endless nights of worry and fear. The bags under her eyes spoke volumes about her exhaustion, and her once-warm smile seemed lost amidst the strain of her current circumstances.

"Ms. Matthews?" Detective Mitchell began, his voice firm yet compassionate. "I'm Detective James Mitchell, and this is Officer Rebecca Johnson. We're here to talk to you about your son, Chosen."

"Please, come in," Melissa said quietly, stepping aside to reveal the cluttered interior of her home. The living room was a mess of discarded clothes, crumpled newspapers, and half-empty mugs—a testament to the chaos that had consumed her life since Chosen's disappearance. Detective Mitchell couldn't help but notice the small, framed photo of a younger Melissa holding baby Chosen, the love and pride in her eyes unmistakable.

"Thank you for seeing us, Ms. Matthews," Officer Johnson said, her tone gentle as she stepped inside. "We know this must be a difficult time for you but we're doing everything we can to find Chosen and bring him home."

"Can you tell us anything about the last time you saw him?" Detective Mitchell asked, observing Melissa closely as she sank into an old armchair, her body language betraying her discomfort.

Melissa's gaze flitted around the room, avoiding eye contact with either of them. "It's been weeks since I last saw him," she admitted, her voice barely above a whisper. "He left one morning and never came back. I've been worried sick ever since."

"Ms. Matthews, we need you to be completely honest with us if we're going to find your son," Detective Mitchell pressed, his eyes locked onto hers, searching for any sign of deceit or evasion.

"Of course," Melissa replied, her voice strained with emotion. "I just want my boy back."

"Trust us, we won't stop until we find him and get to the bottom of this," Officer Johnson promised, her heartfelt sincerity evident in her eyes. Inside, though, she couldn't shake the feeling that there was something more to Melissa's story—and she knew that, one way or another, they would uncover it.

Melissa's pale hands wrung together in her lap, the veins standing out like blue rivers beneath her skin. Her eyes were rimmed with red, a testament to countless sleepless nights spent worrying about Chosen. Detective Mitchell leaned forward slightly, his serious expression never wavering as he began his questioning.

"Ms. Matthews, can you tell us about your relationship with Chosen?" He asked, his voice firm yet measured.

Melissa hesitated, her gaze fixed on a small, frayed hole in the carpet. "Chosen is my whole world," she murmured. "Since the day he was born, I've done everything in my power to give him the best life possible. He's always been a good kid—resourceful and strong-willed but also kind."

"Have you noticed any changes in his behavior recently or any new people he might be associating with?" Detective Mitchell pressed, his eyes scanning Melissa's face for any telling reactions.

A single tear trailed down her cheek, leaving a glistening path in its wake. "No, nothing like that," she replied, her voice cracking with emotion. "He's always been close with his friend Natalie, but other than her, he's never been one to make many friends."

As Melissa spoke, Officer Johnson watched her intently, trying to gauge her sincerity while maintaining a compassionate demeanor. She stepped closer, placing a gentle hand on Melissa's shoulder. "We understand how hard this must be for you, Ms. Matthews. It's clear that you love your son very much," she said softly, her words laced with empathy.

"Thank you," Melissa whispered, her eyes meeting Officer Johnson's for a brief moment before darting away again.

"Is there anything else you can think of that might help us find Chosen?" Detective Mitchell continued, his tone insistent but not unkind. "Any recent arguments or incidents that might have led to his disappearance?"

Melissa's brow furrowed as she searched her memory, attempting to unearth any relevant information. "There was an argument between him and a neighbor a few weeks back but I don't think it amounted to much," she admitted hesitantly. "Chosen is protective of our home and family, so sometimes he gets into conflicts with others."

"Thank you, Ms. Matthews. We'll look into that," Detective Mitchell said, jotting down a note in his small, leather-bound notebook.

As Melissa continued to answer their questions, Officer Johnson couldn't help but feel a growing sense of unease. There was something more to this story—a hidden truth lurking beneath the surface—and it was her job to uncover it. She just hoped they could do so in time to bring Chosen home safely.

Detective Mitchell's gaze sharpened as he studied Melissa, her nervous fidgeting evident in the way she twisted a strand of her wavy brown hair around her finger. A glimmer of sunlight filtered through the broken window, casting a warm glow on her tired face. He knew he had to approach the next line of questioning carefully.

"Ms. Matthews," he began, his voice steady and authoritative. "During our investigation, we discovered some information that may be relevant to Chosen's disappearance. We found records indicating that you gave birth to twins, not just one son."

Melissa's eyes widened and she shook her head vehemently, the strand of hair slipping from her grasp. "No, that's not true. I only have one son, Chosen. He's been missing for weeks now." Her voice trembled with a mix of disbelief and frustration.

Detective Mitchell reached into his jacket pocket and pulled out a worn piece of paper. Unfolding it carefully, he revealed it to be Chosen's birth certificate, along with an attached note mentioning the presence of a twin brother.

"According to this document, Ms. Matthews, Chosen has a twin," he said, his eyes fixed on her reaction.

Melissa stared at the paper, her breath hitching as she tried to make sense of what she was seeing. Her heart pounded in her chest, betraying her otherwise calm exterior. *This can't be right*, she thought, trying to rationalize the situation. *I would know if I had another child.*

"Detective, I don't know why that would be there but I swear I only have one son. Chosen is my world and I would never forget something like that," she insisted, desperation lacing her words.

Officer Johnson watched the exchange with a sympathetic expression, her own thoughts swirling with doubt and confusion. She could see the genuine shock and bewilderment in Melissa's eyes, but was it possible that the woman had suppressed the memory of giving birth to twins? Or was there more to the story they had yet to uncover?

As Detective Mitchell studied Melissa's face, he couldn't shake the nagging feeling that there was a piece of the puzzle still missing. Yet, despite her denial, the evidence presented by the birth certificate was difficult to ignore.

"Ms. Matthews," he said, his voice firm, "we'll need to investigate this further. In the meantime, please let us know if you remember anything else that might help us find Chosen."

Melissa nodded, still unable to comprehend the information she'd just been given. As the detectives left her home, she clutched the doorway for support, her mind racing with thoughts of her missing son, and the possibility of a twin she never knew existed.

Melissa's eyes narrowed as she clutched the birth certificate in her trembling hands, her knuckles turning white. "This can't be right," she insisted, her voice strained.

"Someone must have made a mistake…or worse, it's a forgery."

Detective Mitchell leaned in, his stern gaze locked onto Melissa's face. "Ms. Matthews, we need to consider every possibility. Now, please think. Can you recall any recent conflicts or reasons someone might want to harm Chosen?"

Melissa's thoughts raced, images of Chosen's life flashing through her mind. "I…I don't know," she stammered, her heart pounding in her chest. "Chosen knows how to handle himself on the streets but he's never mentioned any serious trouble."

"Ms. Matthews," Detective Mitchell began, "it's crucial that we understand the circumstances surrounding Chosen's disappearance. Is there anything else you can tell us? Any friends, enemies, or even acquaintances that may provide some insight?"

Melissa's gaze darted around the room as if searching for an answer among the clutter. "He has a best friend, Natalie," she offered hesitantly. "They're inseparable but she wouldn't hurt him. As for enemies…I can't say for sure. Chosen keeps his cards close to his chest."

Detective Mitchell nodded and jotted down the information in his notepad, while Melissa's mind continued to spiral. How could she have forgotten giving birth to twins? And why would the universe conspire to take her only son away from her now?

"Thank you, Ms. Matthews," Detective Mitchell said, closing his notepad. "We'll look into this and keep you informed of any developments."

As the door closed behind the detective, Melissa sank down onto the worn couch, the birth certificate still gripped tightly in her hands. She stared at it, willing the truth to reveal itself but the mystery only deepened. Her thoughts tangled in knots, she wondered what secrets lay hidden in her own past and whether they held the key to finding her missing son.

As Melissa's eyes flickered nervously around the room, the weight of Detective Mitchell's questions seemed to press against her chest. Her hands gripped the crumpled birth certificate more tightly, creasing the edges even further.

"Ms. Matthews," Officer Johnson interjected gently, "You seem quite upset about this." She observed the way Melissa's knuckles whitened as she clung to the paper and the lines of worry etched into her brow.

Melissa's voice trembled as she responded, "I…I just don't understand how this can be true and now…now he's missing."

Detective Mitchell leaned back slightly, allowing Officer Johnson to take the lead. The young officer offered a sympathetic smile, hoping to ease the tension. "We're here to help, Ms. Matthews. Please tell us anything you can think of that might help us find Chosen."

Melissa took a shuddering breath, trying to steady herself. "He was always so strong, so resourceful. He made friends easily but he also made some enemies. There were times when I worried about him getting involved with the wrong crowd, but deep down, I always believed that he could handle whatever life threw at him."

"Did he mention anyone specific?" Officer Johnson asked, watching as Melissa's gaze darted away for a moment before returning to meet her own. A flicker of hesitation, perhaps?

"Uh, no, not really. He didn't talk much about his personal life. But he did mention someone once or twice. I think they had a falling out but I don't know any details."

"Thank you," Officer Johnson said, making a mental note. "We'll do everything we can to bring Chosen home safely."

Melissa's eyes filled with tears, her voice barely a whisper. "I just wish...I wish I could take back certain decisions I made all those years ago. But I swear on my life, I never had twins."

As she spoke, Officer Johnson couldn't help but notice the subtle wavering in her voice and the way her gaze seemed to avoid their own. It wasn't enough to confirm deception but it was enough to raise doubt. With a reassuring nod, she backed away, allowing Detective Mitchell to step forward once more.

"Rest assured, Ms. Matthews, we won't rest until we find Chosen."

Detective Mitchell's eyes narrowed as he took in Melissa's tearful face, the pulsing vein in her temple betraying her stress. Her words and body language didn't quite align; something wasn't adding up. As she clutched the doorframe, he made a decision.

"Officer Johnson," he said, his voice low and authoritative, "I'd like you to dig deeper into Ms. Matthews' background. Double-check any inconsistencies or discrepancies that come up."

"Of course, Detective." Officer Johnson nodded, focusing on the task at hand. She turned back to Melissa, her tone gentle. "Ms. Matthews, we're going to do everything in our power to find Chosen and bring him home safely. We'll need your full cooperation throughout this process."

Melissa's gaze shifted between the two officers, uncertainty flickering in her eyes like a candle flame caught by a draft. "I-I understand," she stammered, her hands trembling slightly.

As Officer Johnson took note of Melissa's unease, her mind raced with thoughts about what could be causing it. Was there another secret lurking beneath the surface? Were they missing a crucial piece of information? She pushed these questions aside for now; first and foremost, they had to focus on finding Chosen.

"Thank you for your cooperation, Ms. Matthews," she said softly, offering a comforting smile. "If you remember anything else or have any new information, please don't hesitate to reach out to us."

Swallowing hard, Melissa nodded. "I will. Please…just find my son."

With a final nod, Detective Mitchell stepped away from the door, his mind already churning with the possibilities and connections forming in his head. There was more to this case—more to Melissa Matthews—than met the eye, and he was determined to uncover the truth, one way or another.

The sun dipped below the horizon as Detective Mitchell pulled the car door closed behind him. The sky, painted in hues of orange and pink, cast a warm glow over Melissa Matthews' dilapidated home. He couldn't shake the feeling that there was more to her story than she had revealed—the denial of having twins, the uncertainty in her eyes. What was she hiding?

"Johnson, we need to look deeper into Melissa's background," he said, his voice firm yet contemplative. "I want you to pull any records you can find on her. Let's see if there are any inconsistencies that might lead us closer to understanding what happened to Chosen."

Officer Johnson nodded; her determination evident in the set of her jaw. "Understood, Detective. I'll start digging as soon as we get back to the station."

As they drove away from the house, the rundown exterior seemed to fade with the setting sun, becoming nothing more than a shadowy outline against the darkening sky. Mitchell glanced at Johnson, noticing how she clenched the steering wheel as her thoughts raced.

"Something bothering you?" He asked, his tone softer than usual.

Officer Johnson hesitated before responding, her gaze fixed on the road ahead. "I just can't help but feel like we're missing something important, some key piece of information that could help us find Chosen."

Mitchell sighed, his eyes narrowing in thought. "I know what you mean. But sometimes, the truth is hidden beneath layers of deception. We'll have to peel them back one by one until we get to the core of this mystery."

They drove in silence for a few moments, the weight of their responsibility hanging heavy in the air between them. Then, Officer Johnson spoke up again, an edge of determination in her voice.

"Melissa loves that boy, it's clear as day. If she's holding something back, it's not because she does not care. Maybe she's just scared."

"Perhaps," Mitchell agreed, his expression contemplative. "But fear can be a powerful motivator, for both good and evil. We must tread carefully as we continue to unravel this tangled web."

With that, the two officers continued their journey back to the station, their minds focused on the task at hand. As they left behind Melissa's home, the shadows of doubt and suspicion grew longer, stretching out like tendrils in pursuit of the truth they sought. And as the last rays of sunlight disappeared from the sky, Detective Mitchell knew one thing for certain: they were far from finished with this case.

Chapter 5

The sound of rain pounded against the windows of the dimly lit interrogation room as Detective James Mitchell and Officer Rebecca Johnson sat across from Ethan, a young man who had been one of the last people to see Chosen based on eyewitness accounts and video footage at the gas station. The cold drizzle did little to deter the pair, the case at hand far more important than the dreary weather.

They both took notes diligently, their pens scratching against paper as Ethan recounted his encounter with Chosen on the night of his disappearance.

"He seemed fine when I saw him," Ethan said, his voice shaky with emotion, "but then he just vanished into thin air. It was like he'd never been there."

Mitchell looked up from his notes, a frown creasing his forehead. "You're sure he didn't go anywhere specific?"

Ethan shook his head. "No, Sir. He was just standing there."

Mitchell stood, tugging at his collar. "We need more expertise on this case," he muttered, glancing out the window at the rain-soaked streets. "Need someone who can help us unravel this mess."

Johnson nodded in agreement, her dark hair swishing behind her as she turned to face him. "Who do you have in mind?"

"Dr. Laura Simmons," Mitchell replied, his eyes distant as he remembered the renowned forensic specialist's previous successes. "She's been known to solve some of the most difficult cases with her uncanny ability to find even the tiniest of clues."

A slurping sound filled the air as they both sipped their hot coffee, the aroma of cinnamon and sugar wafting upwards. The smell mingled with the damp autumn chill that lingered in the air like a ghostly reminder of their unfinished business.

The two detectives stood up, packing their things, and made their way down the station's damp hallways. As they turned the corner, they could hear the faint hum of the copy machine, its warm glow beckoning them toward the evidence room. They entered and found Sgt. Williams, hunched over the machine, making copies of a map that had been discovered with cryptic notes scrawled across it.

"Any luck?" Mitchell asked, walking over to him.

"Not sure, Detective," Sgt. Williams replied, "but it's worth a shot."

Johnson leaned in, her nose wrinkling at the smell of stale coffee and old paper. She could taste the bitterness on her tongue as she studied the map. It looked like whoever drew it knew the town well but was also hiding something.

Mitchell nodded grimly, his gaze flicking to the clock on the wall. "Let's head to Hank's Diner. Maybe someone there knows something about the locations."

They left the station and climbed into their car, the damp autumn air cooling their skin as they drove off into town. The warmth of the car replaced with the crispness outside. Their next stop: Hank's Diner.

Inside, the smell of grease and coffee filled the air. The loud buzz of conversation faded as everyone turned to look at them, their eyes wide with curiosity. Mitchell approached the counter, his voice booming over the clanking of silverware on plates. "Morning, Hank."

The stout man behind the counter nodded, his forehead creased in concern. "What can I do for you two?"

Mitchell produced the map, spreading it out on the counter. "You ever seen this place before? Or any of these locations?"

Hank studied it intently, his bushy eyebrows knitting together. He shook his head slowly. "Nope, can't say I have."

As they turned to go, a woman called out from one of the tables. "Maybe Melissa knows."

They turned toward the source of the voice—an older woman with glasses perched on her nose and a mug of coffee in hand. Johnson approached her, her stomach grumbling at the scent of bacon and eggs. "Hi, Ma'am. Can you tell us more about Melissa?"

The woman frowned, setting her mug down. "She didn't used to be like this," she said slowly. "Something changed after she had that baby. She started locking herself up in the house, acting strange."

"Can you be more specific?" Johnson asked, pen poised over her notepad.

The woman shrugged. "I dunno…just different. Distant. Like she was hiding something."

Johnson made a note of it as Mitchell glanced at his watch. "We need to get moving."

Mitchell's car pulled up to the small house at the end of a winding gravel road, the morning sun glinting off the dusty windshield. They stepped out, their footsteps crunching on the driveway gravel. The house looked abandoned, overgrown shrubs obscuring the windows. The front door creaked open at their knock. A woman stood before them, her hair disheveled and eyes red from crying.

"Mrs. Matthews?" Mitchell asked.

She nodded, sniffling. "What do you want?"

"We need to ask you about your boyfriend's whereabouts on the night of 12 May," Mitchell began.

Her eyes narrowed. "He was here, why?"

Dr. Mark Thompson, a renowned psychological profiler, had been called in to analyze the behavior and motivations of the suspects. He entered the room, his hazel eyes gleaming. "Have you noticed any significant changes in your boyfriend lately, Mrs. Matthews?"

She hesitated, biting her lip. "He's been…distant."

Dr. Simmons, a forensic expert, entered next, her eyes scanning the room. "Anything out of the ordinary around here?"

They all looked around, taking in the cluttered living room with its worn furniture and old newspapers strewn across the floor.

"We've found some suspicious evidence," Mitchell said.

Mrs. Matthews gasped, her eyes widening. "What could that be?"

Dr. Simmons held up a small purple pill bottle. "Prescription medication."

Mrs. Matthews' breath hitched. "That doesn't mean anything."

"It might mean everything," Dr. Thompson countered.

Back at the station, Mitchell sat across from Ethan, his expression serious. "Tell us again what you saw that night."

Ethan ran his hands through his hair, his brow furrowed. "Chosen was arguing with someone…then they disappeared."

Officer Johnson took notes, her pencil moving swiftly across the paper. "Do you know who it was?"

"No," Ethan replied.

The clock ticked loudly on the wall as they talked, the fluorescent lights buzzing overhead. Outside, traffic hummed in the distance. Mitchell glanced at the file on his desk—a photo of Melissa, her eyes cold and hard. He felt a chill run down his spine.

Meanwhile, Ted paced in his kitchen, contemplating his next move. He grabbed a bottle of scotch from the freezer and took a long swig, wincing at the cold burn down his throat.

Dr. Simmons sat in an interrogation room; her eyes focused intently on Mitchell. "The dynamic is crucial here."

Mitchell nodded, taking it all in. "I'll keep that in mind."

Dr. Thompson entered next; his gaze analytical. He glanced at the photos of Chosen and his family before speaking.

In the observation room, they watched Melissa. Her body language spoke volumes: Melissa's arms crossed defensively.

"Something's not adding up," Dr. Thompson whispered.

Dr. Simmons nodded in agreement. "Yes, there's a disconnect."

Natalie Harper was at home, heart racing as she searched for any clue online about her best friend's whereabouts that might help the authorities find him. Her fingers fumbled over the keyboard, desperation growing with each passing second. She took a sip of her lukewarm coffee, tears welling up in her eyes. She had to find him.

Ted walked to his car, his phone buzzing with messages from worried friends and family. By now, everyone had heard about the disappearance of Chosen. Suddenly, his phone vibrated again—a text from Ethan: 'Stay strong'. Ted sighed, wishing things were different.

Meanwhile, Susan was out shopping for groceries for dinner, trying to maintain some sense of normalcy despite the worry gnawing at her gut. She picked up tomatoes, feeling their smooth skin beneath her fingers as she wondered how someone could just disappear like that. Had Chosen run away or met with foul play? Her mind raced with possibilities because it could have easily been her own son missing.

David paced around the living room, deep in thought. The uncertainty was tearing them apart. He couldn't shake the feeling that something wasn't right.

Back at the station, Dr. Simmons and Dr. Thompson's observations resonated with Mitchell. "There's more here than meets the eye," he muttered, eyes locked on the photos of the family. He turned to Natalie's report on Chosen's background, his eyes skimming over details of his difficult childhood protecting Melissa at all costs. "Thank you," he said, handing it back. "This helps."

They walked toward Chosen's neighborhood, the sound of their shoes echoing off the concrete sidewalks. The air was crisp, leaves crunching underfoot. As they approached the park, they spotted Detective Grayson already there, talking on his phone.

"Anything?" Mitchell asked.

"Possible sighting," Grayson replied, looking grim. "Headed toward the woods." The sound of rustling leaves and a distant bark filled the air as they walked toward the trees together, hoping against hope that it wasn't too late.

In the woods, their hearts pounded as they followed the footprints deeper into the brush. They spluttered through puddles and squelched through mud, their boots sucking noisily with each step. The smell of damp earth and rotting leaves filled their nostrils. Suddenly, they heard a twig snap. Everyone stopped, hearts in their throats. "Who's there?" Dr. Simmons called out.

No response. They pressed on, cautiously, until they saw someone huddled under a tree. Tears streamed down his cheeks as he tried to compose himself. "I didn't mean for this to happen," he whispered. His voice trembled as he recounted the events leading up to his disappearance—a stranger offering him a ride, feeling woozy after accepting some candy…it all fell into place now.

Dr. Thompson kneeled beside him, offering a comforting arm around his shoulders. "It's okay, son.

You're safe now. What's your name?" She asked presuming they had located Chosen.

"Michael," the young man replied. She looked up at Mitchell, conveying the need for discretion and care. Whomever this person was, they were clearly shaken up, his eyes darting around anxiously.

Meanwhile, back at Natalie's house, she sat staring at her phone screen. A text from Detective Grayson confirmed her fears: They had found someone but it was not Chosen. She sprang into action—pulling on sneakers, grabbing her keys, and running out the door. Her mind reeled with questions: Who was this stranger? And where was Chosen now?

Natalie ran toward the park entrance, her red curls bouncing behind her. The cool autumn air stung her cheeks as she picked up speed, adrenaline pumping through her veins. She spotted movement ahead and sprinted toward it screaming, "Where's Chosen?"

Someone grabbed her to silence her. "Ma'am, please calm down."

Dr. Simmons came over. "We've found something but it wasn't Chosen," she said grimly, her eyes darkening. "We believe there was foul play involved." Natalie's stomach plummeted; she'd known it all along. But was it connected to threatening notes she'd been receiving? Only time would tell…

The detective asked if she knew anything about any feuds or enemies Chosen might have had. Nothing came to mind except for Ted, but he'd denied any involvement when they questioned him earlier. Natalie gritted her teeth, knowing she had to trust the system now. "Just tell me what you need," she said firmly, determination coursing through her.

As days turned into weeks and weeks into months, there was no sign of Chosen. She visited his mother, Melissa, every day, bringing food and offering support. They were all a mess and seemed to be losing hope. She attended every vigil and rally, hoping someone would come forward with new information. But no one did.

Until one day, while sitting in the park, she saw Officer Johnson chatting to a man she vaguely recognized. He was handing over a file. Her heart hammered in her chest; she knew that look on his face. She approached them cautiously. "Officer Johnson, what's going on?" she asked softly.

She hesitated before meeting her gaze. "We believe your friend might still be alive." Her voice cracked as she spoke, revealing the pain they all felt. "We found some clues that point to…someone close to him." She swallowed hard. "We need your help, Natalie." She nodded, feeling lightheaded.

"I'll do whatever it takes," she whispered, tears welling up in her eyes. They arranged to meet at the station later that day.

As she drove there, her mind raced with questions. Who could be involved? Why would they hurt Chosen? What had she missed? She prayed for answers.

Arriving at the station, she saw Detective Mitchell waiting for her outside his office door, looking grim. "Ms. Harper." He nodded gratefully as she entered. "Thank you for coming." He glanced at the file in her hands; she'd printed out everything she'd found so far. "Please, have a seat."

Officer Johnson entered soon after and pulled out a chair next to her. "So," she began, "you and Chosen, you two know each other?"

"Yeah," Natalie nodded, her voice trembling slightly. "We grew up together."

"Right," Detective Mitchell mused thoughtfully. "Well then you know about his biological family?"

"Yes," Natalie sighed. "Melissa is his mother." She looked down at the file in her lap. "I think there may be more to it but I could not find anything else."

"We believe she might've had something to do with his disappearance," Officer Johnson spoke up. "But we need more evidence."

"Whatever it takes," Natalie repeated. "I'll help."

Detective Mitchell leaned back in his chair. "Ms. Harper, lunch is on us," he said with a small smile. "Let's grab something to eat while we discuss strategy."

At the diner, they ordered burgers and fries, the smell of grease filling the air as they shared their thoughts on how they could find more information about Melissa. Natalie mentioned a guy named Zeke who had recently gotten out of jail and had been seen lurking around Chosen's old neighborhood. "He used to be a friend of Chosen's," she explained anxiously. "But things turned sour when Melissa started dating his father."

The officers exchanged glances; then Detective Mitchell spoke up. "We'll look into it."

Over lunch, they brainstormed about potentially bringing in more experts who might help them understand the complex family dynamics better.

Officer Johnson added, "Dr. Simmons and Dr. Thompson are at the top of their respective fields and should be all we need for now," nodding toward her own file. "Dr. Thompson is a forensic pathologist—he could assist with the medical aspect. Dr. Simmons could provide valuable insight with her expertise, as well."

"Good thinking," Detective Mitchell responded. "We'll see if we can get them both officially on board."

As they finished up lunch, Natalie's stomach churned with nervous energy. She wanted to do more but wasn't sure what that was. Driving home, she stopped by Chosen's favorite coffee shop, hoping someone might've seen him. The barista remembered him vividly: "He always got an espresso shot with extra foam," he said. Natalie scribbled down notes in her notebook while chatting about Chosen's likes and dislikes. It wasn't much but every bit helped.

Natalie ran to her car and dialed Detective Mitchell's number. "It's me," she stated urgently. "I have some info that might help." She shared what she'd learned about Zeke and mentioned Dr. Simmons and Dr. Thompson's potential involvement.

Detective Mitchell's voice was excited. "Great work, Natalie! We'll reach out to them both."

She ended the call, feeling accomplished but anxious about what might come next. Visiting Zeke was risky—she wasn't sure if he'd cooperate—but it was worth a try. Her stomach churned with nerves as she stepped out of her car and approached his trailer park home. The place reeked of stale cigarettes and desperation; flies buzzed around an old TV playing a game show inside. She knocked on the door, heart pounding like a drum.

Zeke answered, his eyes wary yet curious. She introduced herself and asked if he'd seen Chosen recently. He shook his head slowly, looking away. "Not since before his mom started seeing my old man," he muttered. "Why?"

Natalie took a deep breath. "We just want to know he's safe," she lied. "Can you confirm that?"

Zeke scrunched up his face in thought, then shrugged nonchalantly.

Relief washed over her. They had a lead. Zeke didn't seem suspicious about her motives; she hoped it stayed that way. She thanked him and left, her head spinning with questions: Where had Chosen gone? And who was he with?

Back in her car, she typed out messages to Dr. Simmons and Detective Mitchell, filling them in on the new details. An hour later, they replied: they'd agreed to meet for an update. Her heart raced as she drove there, wondering what they might find.

Arriving at Chosen's place, she found Dr. Simmons pacing outside Melissa's home while Detective Mitchell examined the scene inside. They both turned to her in unison as she pulled up. Their eyes were full of anticipation mixed with concern.

"Good work, Natalie." Dr. Simmons smiled warmly. "What did you find out?"

Natalie swallowed hard. "I spoke with Zeke," she began. "He may have seen."

Dr. Mitchell nodded slowly. "Good work," he said before entering Melissa's. He emerged a moment later with a grim look on his face. "Inconsistencies," he muttered under his breath. "The place has been cleaned up, too much."

Dr. Simmons furrowed her brow. "Smells like bleach," she noted, sniffing the air. "As if someone was trying to cover up any trace of struggle or foul play."

Natalie's stomach sank. This wasn't good. "We need more help than I can give," she admitted. "I'm not a professional."

Dr. Simmons's eyes softened. "We understand, sweetie. That's why we're here." She placed a reassuring hand on her shoulder. "Let's review everything you've found so far."

Natalie recounted her visits to Chosen's usual haunts: the gym, the coffee shop down the street, his favorite park bench. She told them about Ethan, who claimed to have seen someone arguing with Chosen before he vanished. As she spoke, Detective Mitchell scribbled down notes on his pad and Dr. Simmons nodded thoughtfully.

"This Ethan character," he said finally. "Do you think we can track him down?"

Natalie nodded eagerly. "I think so."

The three of them drove to the university together, where they spoke with Ethan in one of the professors' lounges. His story—a lie—remained consistent: a man in a dark hoodie arguing with Chosen. The sketch artist helped capture an image of the suspect from Ethan's memory and it sent a chill down Natalie's spine. It looked like the man from Melissa's nightmares.

As they drove back to the police station, Natalie felt a weight lift from her shoulders. For the first time, she felt like they were getting somewhere. "We need to find this guy," she said determinedly.

Detective Mitchell glanced at her. "We will," He promised. "But we could use your help." He paused. "We're not doing this alone."

Natalie hesitated, unsure what to say. She wanted to trust them but ever since Chosen disappeared, she'd been wary of anyone claiming to help.

"We just want to find your friend," Officer Johnson added softly. "We want to solve this case as much as you do."

Natalie bit her lip, then nodded slowly. "Okay," she finally agreed. "What do you want me to do?"

Detective Mitchell handed her a stack of photos. "Start by going door-to-door in the areas where Chosen frequented. See if anyone recognizes this man." She took the pictures from him and flipped through them, her heart racing. This was it—she could really make a difference.

Over the next few days, Natalie hit the pavement hard, showing the pictures to business owners and residents alike. The air was crisp and the leaves crunched beneath her shoes as she walked down the sidewalks. The scent of pumpkin spice lattes filled the air from the coffee shop where Chosen loved to write. It was strange being there without him. But she pushed on, driven by a newfound resolve.

Finally, at a grocery store near Chosen's apartment, she struck gold. An elderly woman recognized the man in the photos from a recent robbery at a nearby bank. The suspect had been caught on camera. Detective Mitchell and Officer Johnson rushed to the bank, where they interviewed the teller and examined the security footage. They were elated at the break in the case.

Back at the station, Dr. Simmons and Dr. Thompson were going over a related report. "This is fascinating," Dr. Simmons said, his eyes glinting with interest. "So many layers to unravel here." Dr. Thompson nodded in agreement, his glasses fogging up slightly as he leaned in to study the file.

Natalie sat in the waiting room, tapping her foot impatiently. She couldn't stand being away from the action anymore. Finally, Detective Mitchell emerged, his face grim. "We found something," he said, pulling her into his office. "Come take a look at this."

They showed her the security footage of the man who grabbed Chosen outside the bank. "We believe he's responsible for Chosen's disappearance," he explained. "But we need to track him down." Natalie felt a surge of adrenaline course through her veins. She had to help them.

She took a deep breath and shared what she knew about the robbery suspect from her own investigation. "He was spotted at the grocery store too," she added.

Detective Mitchell's eyes widened. "Excellent work, Miss Harper. You could potentially be our missing piece in this puzzle." He turned to Officer Johnson. "Let's pay that store another visit."

As they drove to the grocery store, Officer Johnson turned to her. "You sure you're ok with this, Miss Harper?"

"Absolutely," she said, her heart pounding with excitement.

Inside the store, they split up; Natalie heading toward the checkout where she'd seen the suspect, while Officer Johnson and Detective Mitchell checked the parking lot. Natalie's heart skipped a beat as she recognized the brand of gum he'd been eating. She ran to the store manager. "The brand of gum he was chewing," she said urgently. The manager nodded and they rushed back to the car.

They traced the gum wrapper back to a factory, finding a lead that led them to a warehouse. It was eerily silent as they approached. Suddenly, shots rang out. A woman screamed and they dove for cover. Over the sound of gunfire, Natalie caught a glimpse of a figure darting away into the darkness. As the shooting subsided, they cautiously advanced, finding the robbery suspect dead.

Detective Mitchell swore under his breath. "This is getting messier by the minute." He radioed for backup but they knew they couldn't wait.

Natalie's stomach churned. They searched the warehouse, finding clues that pointed to a larger criminal organization's involvement. "We need to bring in some more resources," Detective Mitchell said, making the call.

Amid the chaos, Natalie's eyes locked with Officer Johnson's; they both knew they couldn't do this alone. As the crime scene techs arrived, they filled them in on what they had found so far. Officer Johnson nodded; her eyes fierce with determination. "We'll follow every lead," she promised.

That night, Dr. Simmons joined them for a strategy session at the police station. They pored over evidence, brainstorming theories and suspects. "What about Melissa's ex-boyfriend?" Natalie suggested hesitantly. Everyone turned to look at her. "He was abusive," she explained quietly.

Dr. Thompson, a forensic psychologist, frowned deeply. "Worth looking into," he agreed.

Detective Mitchell tapped his pen against his chin. "We'll bring him in for questioning."

As they worked late into the night, exhaustion set in. Officer Johnson ordered pizza for everyone and they shared stories over pepperoni and soda. The camaraderie was surprising; they were all in this together now.

Days turned into weeks, and leads came and went without any sign of Chosen. The case was splashed across the news frequently, causing distress for Chosen's birth mother, Melissa. She was torn between guilt and worry, and blame began to simmer beneath the surface as well.

Natalie felt it too; she couldn't shake the niggling feeling that she was missing something critical. She decided to visit Melissa again, this time with Detective Mitchell. They found her at home, eyes red from crying, looking frazzled but hopeful. She told them about a recent argument with Chosen over money before he disappeared. It didn't add up…

Chapter 6

Detective James Mitchell and Officer Rebecca Johnson pulled up to the Greenfield police station, a modest building tucked away in the heart of the small town. As they stepped out of the car, the crisp fall air hit their faces and the sound of leaves rustling beneath their feet echoed through the quiet streets.

The town's quaint atmosphere was palpable; painted houses lined up like a picture-perfect postcard, with well-manicured lawns and friendly faces peeking out from behind curtains. A sense of community was strong here, something that Mitchell had rarely seen in his years working in the big city.

The inside of the station was no different. The officer on duty gave them a warm smile as they introduced themselves, offering them coffee that smelled of freshly ground beans. The room was cozy, with old-fashioned lamps casting a warm glow over the worn wooden desk. They were led to a back room where files were meticulously organized, dusty with age but well-kept. The officer began to pull out the relevant documents on the Thompsons' adoption, flipping through each page carefully.

While she searched, Mitchell glanced around the room, taking in the familiar sights and sounds. The ticking of an old clock on the wall, the rustle of paper as they went through the files, the occasional tap of fingers against the desktop as they made notes. He noticed a framed picture on the officer's desk, a family photo, likely taken recently by the looks of it. Another family, another life, he thought, feeling a pang of nostalgia for his own family back home.

Officer Johnson pulled out the folder and laid it on the desk, her brow furrowed in concentration as she read through the information. Her fingers traced over the words, emphasizing certain names and dates as she scanned the pages. She let out a soft sigh, "This is going to take some time." Mitchell nodded in agreement, leaning over her shoulder to get a better look.

As they pored over the adoption records, the room fell silent except for the occasional shuffling of paper and the clicking of keys as the officer typed in information into their system. The smell of fresh-brewed coffee filled the air, mingling with the musty scent of old files and ink. Outside, the wind picked up, causing the blinds to rattle against the windowpane. The town clock struck noon, signaling lunchtime for many of the local residents.

"Let's grab a bite," suggested Mitchell. "It'll give us a chance to chat with some locals, see if we can gather any other information about the Thompsons."

Officer Johnson nodded enthusiastically, eager to get to know more about the close-knit community. Together they walked down Main Street, past the bakery where the aroma of freshly baked bread and pies wafted out onto the sidewalk. People greeted them with waves and smiles, stopping to talk about the weather and the latest gossip. It was clear this town loved its gossip.

They settled into a cozy diner; their plates piled high with homemade comfort food.

"So, tell me about yourself," said Mitchell between bites of his burger. "What brought you to our department?"

"A mix of reasons," replied Officer Johnson, taking a sip of her iced tea. "Looking for a slower pace, wanted to start fresh after some personal stuff back home."

As they ate, they discussed the case, debating theories and possibilities. Both were curious about Ted Thompson, Ethan's childhood friend who had grown up with Chosen but led a much different life. They wondered if there was any connection between the two brothers and if Ted had any role in Chosen's disappearance.

Back outside, they resumed their investigation by visiting neighbors of the Thompsons. Mrs. Davis, an elderly lady who lived two doors down, remembered Ted playing in her yard when he was younger. She smiled fondly at the memory but grew serious when mentioning how quiet things had been lately. She hadn't seen Ted in months. "It's quite unlike him," she said, shaking her head. "He used to be such a social butterfly."

Detective Mitchell followed up on a hunch and visited the local library, where he found Melissa studying alone. She looked up when he approached her desk, startled by the sudden interruption. Her eyes widened in recognition before she quickly looked away, shaking her head no. Something told him she was lying.

"I've been here since early morning," she said, biting her lip nervously. "I didn't see anything out of the ordinary."

Her fingers tap-tap-tapped against the keyboard as if drumming out a nervous tune while she scrolled through something on her laptop screen. He noticed an open tab with an adoption website on it. She seemed evasive and guarded; there might be something else going on here.

As they left, they ran into their sergeant who asked about their progress so far. Both officers reported that they had some leads but nothing concrete yet. They decided to visit the Thompson house again.

As they approached, the house seemed eerily quiet—no lawnmowers or kids playing nearby. The freshly cut grass smelled sweet underfoot as they knocked on the door. A gust of wind blew through, rustling leaves and carrying faint laughter from down the street.

The Thompsons answered, looking drawn and tired. They invited them inside, offering cool drinks and sweaty orange slices for the warm day. Detective Mitchell noticed Ted sitting alone in the living room, staring off into the distance.

"Ted, do you remember anything about your birth family?" He asked gently, taking a seat beside him.

He shook his head slowly, his voice barely above a whisper. "I wish I did...I wish I could help find my brother."

Officer Johnson noticed Mrs. Thompson's eyes dart toward the hallway before quickly looking away. Something was off but she couldn't quite put her finger on it yet.

They talked for a while longer before leaving, promising to stay in touch if anyone remembered anything useful. Back in the car, they pored over their notes. Officer Johnson couldn't shake the feeling that something wasn't adding up about this family.

As they left, Detective Mitchell couldn't help but wonder what else Melissa was hiding.

Back at the library, the scent of old books and freshly brewed coffee filled the air. A poster for a local support group caught their eye: 'Adoptive Parents United'. They decided to attend the next meeting, hoping to strike gold with someone who might know something about the Thompsons' adoption process. The attendees were small but close-knit, all eager to share their stories over cups of hot cocoa.

They listened intently as several parents spoke about their journeys to parenthood and the joy of finding their forever children. A middle-aged woman, her hair pulled back in a tight bun, mentioned a closed adoption she'd been part of a few years prior. "The Thompsons…they attended a few meetings," she said between sips of her drink. "Very private people, they kept to themselves."

It was worth a shot.

Next stop, the Thompsons' extended family—cousins, aunts, and uncles—all of them called in for questioning. The familial bond was clear as they chatted about old times over tea and biscuits, sharing stories of birthdays and holidays spent together. But no one had any concrete information about the adoption. As they wrapped up, Officer Johnson noticed a framed photo on the mantle: two young boys, smiling brightly under the sea at a tropical destination.

"Do you mind if I take a look?" She asked politely, holding out her hand. One of the uncles handed it over without hesitation.

Inspecting the photo more closely, she saw the date: ten years ago. The boys looked so much alike—identical even in their grins. "Do either of these boys resemble Melissa?" She asked softly, showing the picture to Detective Mitchell who had been outside chatting with another relative.

He squinted, leaning in for a better look. "Hard to say from this angle, but maybe…" His voice trailed off as he took the photo to get a better look. "Could it be possible that Ted was the twin?"

The room went silent. A million thoughts raced through Officer Johnson's mind as they left the house and drove back to the station. She couldn't shake the image of those bright smiles from her mind or the feeling that something wasn't quite right about this whole situation. They needed to dig deeper into the Thompsons' past.

Back at the station, they poured over every scrap of paper they had on the case, trying to connect any dots they'd missed before. The adoption agency had been thorough but was there anything they'd missed? A hint of desperation lurked in the air, like a dark cloud following them both. Detective Mitchell couldn't shake off the feeling that Melissa was hiding something big, his gut telling him she was involved somehow.

Officer Johnson sat in silence, piecing together the scattered clues—the sealed records, the photos of Chosen, Melissa's guilty demeanor during interrogation. It all felt too coincidental now. They needed more evidence, more proof.

As night fell, they agreed to pay another visit to the Thompsons, this time with backup and search warrants in hand. They were determined. With a deep breath, Officer Johnson grabbed her coat and left for another long night of sleuthing.

The hospital was cold and quiet, their footsteps echoing down the empty halls. The nurses on duty were helpful but guarded, not wanting to divulge any information about patients without a warrant. Detective Mitchell showed his badge and explained their situation, the missing twin and the Thompsons' connection. The hospital staff reluctantly led them to the maternity ward where Ted Thompson was born.

The air smelled of disinfectant and medicine, making Officer Johnson's nose wrinkle in discomfort. She scanned the rooms, each one looking like the last, until she overheard a voice—a familiar one. It was the woman who denied having twins initially, Melissa Matthews. Her heart sank as she realized they might be onto something big.

Detective Mitchell followed her gaze and saw the same woman, tears streaming down her face. He approached her cautiously, his gut telling him this would be a breakthrough. He showed her his badge and asked if she could help them find her son. She looked at him through watery eyes, "I want to tell you everything, Detective."

In a small room off the main corridor, they sat and listened to Melissa's confession. The adoption agency had pressured her into giving up one of her twins, insisting that they couldn't let both go. They'd promised to keep the other child safe and secret but she'd always wondered if they'd kept their word. At first, she didn't know who had adopted him or where he was. Later, she found the adopted family and contacted them.

The twin she gave up was Ted Thompson, identical twin brother of the twin she kept who is now missing—Chosen. The detective took notes frantically as she spoke, his pencil scratching against the notepad like a hungry animal looking for food. He looked at Officer Johnson, who nodded determinedly, signaling she'd get on it.

Leaving Melissa in the care of a nurse, they went back to the main ward, their feet echoing on the cold floor. They stopped at the nurses' station and Johnson started asking around about any records from that time period. There were none left but one nurse remembered something from the day Ted and Chosen were born. A young woman, not a mother, had been asking questions about the babies. She was persistent, wanting to know when any would be ready for adoption. It didn't sit right with her at the time but she'd shrugged it off as curiosity.

But now? Now it could be important. They thanked her and headed out the door, back to their car. As they drove to the adoption agency, they shared a look of anticipation mixed with fear. What if this lead went nowhere? What if they'd never find Chosen?

Arriving at the agency, they met with the director who seemed nervous but happy to help. He pulled out old files, flicking through yellowing pages until he found what they were looking for—the adoption papers for the Matthews twins. He hesitated before handing them over, saying there might be something else they should see. Something that could help them find Chosen.

Entering another room, they found a small box with an old camera inside. Inside that were photos of the twins but one was missing. In its place, a photo of Chosen. Their hearts raced as they recognized his features and stared at the tiny handwriting on the back: "To whoever finds him, here's my secret. He's not who you think he is."

Suddenly, it all clicked. They rushed back to the hospital to speak with the former employee from before. Her name was Grace Henderson. She looked older now, her eyes sunken and tired from years of guilt. She told them everything she knew, starting from the moment she'd seen Chosen in the dumpster to the moment she'd left town after reporting it to her superiors.

She'd been harboring this secret all these years, worried she'd done something wrong by not reporting it sooner. But now she knew it could help bring closure and justice for Chosen.

As Detective Mitchell listened intently, he noticed Officer Johnson scribbling down details on a notepad while also wearing a determined expression on her face. A look of determination that mirrored his own. They left the hospital, their next stop: the orphanage where Ted had been taken from.

The rain pattered against the car windows as they drove, their minds whirring with theories and questions. Could this be it? Would they finally find out what happened? The car door shut with a loud click as they stepped out into the cold air, leaving behind another clue closer to uncovering the truth.

Inside the orphanage, they found an old woman who remembered everything about that fateful day years ago—

the look on Ted's face as he was taken away, the sound of his cries echoing down the halls. But there was something else too—a scent lingered in the air, like freshly baked cookies. It reminded them both of home and made them feel a little less alone in this sea of uncertainty.

The woman led them to the files room where they pored over paperwork from the adoption agency, carefully crossing off names until they reached one that stood out: Mr. and Mrs. Thompson. The date matched up; it was the same day Ted had been taken from the orphanage. There had to be some connection here.

But still, they needed more proof. Back at the station, they called Melissa in for questioning once again. Her carefully constructed stories began to unravel under their persistent probing. She seemed anxious, her hands trembling slightly as she picked at her nails.

"I...I don't know what you're talking about," she stuttered when asked about the adoption agency employee who'd come forward. "I never met her."

Mitchell believed her but something didn't add up. He glanced over at Officer Johnson who nodded in agreement— they needed to dig deeper.

The clock struck 4 pm when they finally decided to visit the agency themselves. Raindrops drummed against the roof of their car as they pulled up outside its worn-down facade. A sign outside read 'Adoptions Incorporated, Established 1972'. Inside, a musty scent hit them—old papers and yellowing files.

The receptionist looked up, surprised to see them but led them to an office where an older woman sat behind a desk.

She was thin, her hair pulled back into a tight bun, eyes darting around nervously.

"Mrs. Broadmoor? We have some questions for you." Mitchell began, his voice steady despite the growing suspicion in his chest. A fleeting look of panic crossed her face before she stood up and bolted for the door—catching a glimpse of her file cabinet labeled 'Classified'.

They sprung after her, finding the door locked.

"You don't want to do this!" She cried, her voice echoing in the hallway. "They'll come for you too!"

Mitchell pulled out his phone, calling for backup as Officer Johnson tried the knob. Click. The sound of the lock giving way filled the silent hallway.

Inside, they found a hidden room filled with boxes labeled 'Adoptions Gone Wrong'. Each one contained evidence of children—pictures, reports, even DNA samples.

But one file stood out…Ted's.

The papers rattled as Mitchell flipped through them—photos of the happy family, medical records, even a picture of the birth mother. She looked familiar…

They recognized her. It was Melissa.

A shiver ran down his spine. This was getting personal.

Rebecca's stomach churned at the sight of it all. She couldn't help but think of her own brother who'd been taken from her as a child. This agency was hiding more than they were letting on.

They left Greenfield with a renewed sense of determination, ready to uncover the secrets and mysteries surrounding the Thompsons' adoption and the whereabouts of Chosen. They knew they were onto something big.

The wind whistled through open windows as they drove away from the agency, blurring scenery passing by in a flurry of colors and shapes. Their minds raced with all they'd seen and heard. The case was growing darker by the second but they were closer to justice.

"Let's talk to Ethan again," Rebecca suggested, flipping on the sirens to make haste. "He might have more answers."

Ethan sat at a diner alone, nursing a cup of coffee. His eyes lit up when he saw them walk in, worried.

"I didn't do anything wrong, did I?" He asked nervously.

"Not at all," Rebecca reassured him. "We just have some new leads. Anything you can tell us about the Thompsons would be helpful."

He took a sip of his coffee, clearing his throat. "There is not much to say."

Detective Mitchell made a note on his notepad. "What about the mother? Does she seem suspicious to you?"

He shook his head. "Nope. But then again, who knows what people are really thinking?"

They both couldn't help but agree. People could be good at hiding their true feelings.

Back at the station, they grilled Melissa Matthews again about her boyfriend's work. She repeated the same story she had told them before, trying to keep her composure amidst their growing suspicion. It was becoming obvious that she was lying about something. But what?

A knock on the door interrupted their thoughts. A man in a trench coat walked in, holding a package. "This was left under the mailbox," he said quietly. "Thought you'd want it."

Detective Mitchell's eyes widened as he opened the box; inside were pictures of Chosen as a baby. He quickly flipped through them, feeling his stomach drop. There were pictures of the twins together, taken before they were separated. And in the background…was it possible? Was it a glimpse of Melissa holding both babies?

"She lied," Mitchell muttered, showing the images to Rebecca. "Let's pay her another visit."

Chapter 7

The room was quiet, almost too quiet. The fluorescent lights buzzed overhead as Officers Rebecca Johnson and Nate Norman sat at the small table in the interrogation room, their hands wrapped around hot cups of black coffee. The officer took a deep breath, letting out a slow sigh as she leaned back in her chair. "It's been one hell of a day, hasn't it?" She asked, her eyes tired but earnest. Officer Norman nodded in agreement, taking a sip from his own cup before setting it down on the scratched surface of the table.

"I don't think I've ever seen anything like it," he replied, running a hand through his short blonde hair and pushing back the slight sheen of sweat from his forehead. His lean build was tense under his worn t-shirt and he couldn't help but rub at the small knot forming between his shoulders. He glanced over at Rebecca, noticing how her long dark hair fell around her face as she leaned forward, elbows on the table. "You know, this case…it's really gotten to me."

She looked up at him, her green eyes meeting his brown ones. There was an understanding there, a bond that they had formed throughout the day that went beyond their professional duties. "It's tough. Chosen seemed to be a decent guy," her voice trailed off as she shook her head slightly, trying to push away the image from her mind.

They sat in silence for a moment, each lost in their thoughts as the fluorescent lights hummed overhead. The smell of coffee and old donuts lingered in the air, mixed with the faint aroma of stale cigarettes from outside. The sound of their breathing was the only thing breaking the silence until Officer Norman broke it. "Do you want to grab dinner somewhere? My treat."

Rebecca hesitated for a moment before nodding. "Yeah, that sounds great." She stood up, stretching her arms over her head and Officer Norman could see the muscles in her back ripple under her uniform shirt.

Outside, the night air was cool and they walked briskly toward a nearby Italian place. The neon signs flickered above them, casting a warm glow on their faces as they navigated through the bustling city streets. The sound of car horns and people laughing echoed around them, but neither paid much attention as they made their way to their destination. Once inside, they took a seat by the window, the warm light of the restaurant casting shadows across their table.

As they placed their orders, Officer Norman couldn't help but notice the way Rebecca's eyes darted around the room, taking everything in—the waiters, the other patrons, even the kitchen staff. He knew she was always on high alert, always ready for anything. When their food arrived, they dug in with the same vigor they had tackled the case earlier. The tangy sauce coated their tongues and the soft noodles melted in their mouths, but neither could seem to shake the feeling that something wasn't quite right...

The sound of a car door slamming outside sent adrenaline rushing through them both and they knew their night wasn't over yet.

After dinner, they walked back to the station in silence, their footsteps echoing on the pavement. The sound of a car door slamming outside sent adrenaline rushing through them both, it was too late for this to be coincidental. As they approached the building, they heard shouting and sirens in the distance. Their hearts racing, they instinctively slowed down as they rounded the corner, and that's when they saw it.

The crime scene tape was stretched across the front door of an apartment building. Officers swarmed around the entrance like ants on a sugar cube, talking animatedly among themselves. Rebecca's eyes met Nate's—weary but determined—and without hesitation, they pushed through the crowd toward the commotion. "What happened?" She asked, her voice sharp with urgency.

A uniformed officer looked up at her, his face pale. "Another murder," he muttered, shaking his head. "We found another body."

Rebecca's stomach dropped. She nodded grimly and pushed past him into the building, Nate right behind her. The stench of death hit them like a wall—metallic blood and sweat mingled with the stale air from the stairwell. They climbed the steps slowly, each breath a struggle against the suffocating smell. At the top, they saw a lifeless form sprawled out on the floor, blood pooling around him. Nate's heart sank; this wasn't just a murder; it was personal.

They spent hours poring over the evidence, questioning neighbors and trying to piece together what could have happened. By the time they left, it was dark outside and they were both emotionally exhausted. They drove to the station in silence, each lost in their own thoughts about what they had just witnessed. When they finally made it to the station, they breathed a sigh of relief at seeing the familiar, fluorescent lit halls. Nate grabbed a coffee from the break room, then led her to an empty interrogation room to debrief.

As they sat down, they couldn't help but glance at each other—both had seen too much today, both had felt too much. "It's tough, isn't it?" Nate finally broke the silence. "Being so close to all this violence?"

Rebecca nodded grimly, taking a sip of her own cup of coffee. It was lukewarm but she didn't care; any warmth would do right now. "I don't know how you do it," she admitted softly.

Nate shrugged, looking away. "I guess it's just who we are." He paused for a moment, "You can be pretty tough too, though. You've got guts."

A blush crept up Rebecca's cheeks at his compliment. She took another sip of coffee but avoided his gaze. "Thanks," she mumbled, her voice still rough from the emotions of the day.

They sat together in the quiet room, sipping their coffees slowly as they tried to process everything that had happened.

Suddenly, Nate leaned over the table and his lips met hers—soft and tentative at first, then more urgently. She responded eagerly, their tongues dancing together in a desperate tango of need and desire. Their hands found each other's hair, tangling in the curls and holding on tight. The sound of their kiss was loud in the small room, the slurp of coffee being forgotten as they became lost in each other.

Nate pulled away, panting slightly. "I've…I've wanted this for so long," he confessed, his eyes searching hers.

"Me too," she managed to whisper between gasps.

Their kiss deepened once more, their emotions spilling over into the act. It was as if they were drowning in each other's touch, their connection growing stronger by the moment.

Suddenly, the sound of the ringing phone on Detective Mitchell's desk broke through the fog of their passion. The detective cursed under his breath as he answered it next door, the spell broken. "It's about the case," he muttered, his voice tense. "We need to get back out there."

Reluctantly, they pulled apart, both feeling slightly disoriented from the intensity of their moment. As they stood up, their eyes locked, communicating their reluctance to leave this haven of passion behind.

Johnson nodded slowly, her cheeks flushed with desire. "Let's go," she managed to say, grabbing her jacket off the back of the chair.

The cold air hit them as they stepped outside, bringing with it the familiar smell of coffee and pizza from the local joint near the precinct. The city buzzed around them, people going about their lives unaware of the danger lurking beneath the surface. They climbed into her car, both trying to regain their bearings after the heat of their encounter.

"I just want you to know," Nate started, his hand finding hers on the gearshift. "This isn't just a fling for me. I really care about you, Becca."

She turned to look at him, her face softening. "I know," she replied, squeezing his hand. "I feel the same way."

As they drove back to the precinct, their minds wandered back to Chosen's case, the mystery still unsolved. Their hearts ached for the young man and they knew they had to find his killer. Detective Mitchell was waiting for them when they arrived, his expression grim.

"We got a lead on a possible suspect," he announced as they walked in. "A man with a grudge against Melissa. Let's go see what he knows."

Their hearts raced, hopeful that this would be the break they needed. Little did they know, they were walking into a web of deceit and danger that would change their lives forever.

In the interrogation room, the suspect sat calmly, smirking at them from behind his cuffs. "So, you think I did it?" He sneered.

"We just want to ask you some questions," Detective Mitchell said, taking a seat across from him. "You had a fight with Melissa recently, didn't you?"

The man shifted in his chair. "Yeah, but I didn't kill no one."

"Why did you fight?" Officer Johnson prodded.

"She owes me money," he spat. "She's a damn liar and a cheat."

"What makes you say that?" Mitchell asked, leaning forward.

"I caught her stealing from me," he said, his voice low. "I warned her to stay away but she kept coming back."

They exchanged glances, this new information sending shockwaves through them. Was Melissa capable of such deceit?

As they left the interrogation room, Officer Johnson turned to Detective Mitchell. "Do you think there's any truth to this?"

He nodded slowly. "Let's check it out."

They drove to Melissa's house, tension thick in the air. Nate's stomach churned as they walked up to the door, remembering their passionate kiss only hours ago. What if she was involved? They knocked and Melissa answered, looking surprised to see them.

"Hi, Detective Mitchell, Officer Johnson," she said warily. "What can I do for you?"

"Mind if we come in?" Detective Mitchell asked, his tone firm.

She hesitated but stepped back, allowing them entry. There were what appeared to be signs of struggle— overturned furniture, broken dishes, empty bottles scattered about. It looked like a fight had taken place here too. "What's going on?" She asked, eyes wide with fear.

They questioned her about the allegations and she broke down, confessing to stealing from him but insisting she never hurt anyone.

"I didn't kill my son," she cried, her voice breaking. "I would never hurt Chosen."

Officer Johnson bit her lip, not sure what to believe anymore. They continued searching, finding nothing incriminating against Melissa but growing more suspicious of everyone else they interviewed.

Back at the station, Officer Norman and Officer Johnson compared notes over coffee. They both looked drained, their professional facades slipping as they stole glances at each other across the table. The taste of the bitter brew lingered on their tongues, reminding them of the harsh reality they were dealing with. A lead came in about a possible suspect, and they sprang into action, following it up eagerly.

The air was cool outside as they walked toward the address, their footsteps echoing on the pavement. The sound of sirens in the distance made Officer Johnson's heart race. What if they were headed toward Chosen's location? What if it was too late?

They arrived at the warehouse, hearts pounding in their chests. The door creaked open, revealing a dimly lit room filled with boxes and tools of the trade. Their breath caught in their throats when they saw someone, tied up and gagged on the other side of the room. Relief washed over them as they rushed over to free him, asking questions quickly.

"We heard there was an intruder here," he said between gasps for air. "A woman…she took something important of mine." His voice trembled as he pointed toward a box in the corner. Inside was a key; the key to everything.

The adrenaline rush wore off quickly, leaving them both shaken but determined. They searched for clues, combing through the boxes and peering under every nook and cranny. Their hands brushed against each other accidentally more than once, sending tingles up their spines.

As night fell, they decided to call it a night and head back to the station. Their senses were on high alert as they drove back, their eyes constantly scanning the streets for any sign of movement. Officer Johnson's car smelled of coffee and sweat from their earlier run. She was exhausted but couldn't seem to let go of Chosen's face.

"I thought I'd lost you," Officer Norman whispered, reaching over to hold her hand. Hers trembled slightly in his grasp.

"Same here," she responded softly, squeezing his hand tightly.

Once they got to the station, they found themselves alone in a car talking about what had just happened. The words flowed freely between them and they found solace in each other's company.

"I don't know how you manage to be so calm in these situations," Nate said with admiration in his voice.

She shrugged modestly, "I guess I've always been good at connecting with people."

He looked at her intently, his piercing blue eyes searching hers. "You're really something," he murmured.

Their bodies inched closer as they spoke, the silence between them thick with unspoken emotions. Finally, they shared a tender kiss that lingered long after it ended. Nate pulled back reluctantly, his heart pounding in his chest. "This can't happen again," he warned her seriously.

"I know," she agreed, trying to control the butterflies in her stomach. She turned on the ignition and started the engine, her fingers brushing against his again.

The late-night city lights cast a warm glow over their faces as they drove off into the darkness, both consumed by their thoughts and their growing feelings for each other. They knew they had to be careful but something about this connection felt too strong to ignore.

Back at the station, they sat at their desks, lost in thought until Detective Mitchell walked in, breaking the spell. "Good job tonight, you two," he said with a hint of a smile. "We'll compare notes in the morning."

Officer Johnson smiled back at him; her cheeks flushed from their secret exchange. Officer Norman nodded silently, his mind still reeling from the events of the day. The two of them retreated to their respective squad cars for the night, unable to sleep due to the adrenaline rush and the pull they felt toward each other.

The next morning, they arrived at the station early, eager to piece together their findings from the stakeout. The cold coffee from the break room didn't taste as bitter as it usually did; instead, it brought back memories of the intimate moments they shared last night. They exchanged glances throughout the meeting, their hearts racing every time their eyes met.

As they walked back to their desks, Detective Mitchell approached them, holding a photo of the suspect they were after. "We got him," he said proudly. "He was caught red-handed."

With a sigh of relief, butterflies fluttered excitedly in both their stomachs.

"Can I ask you something?" Officer Johnson whispered to Officer Norman when they were alone. "I know it's not related but I need to get it off my chest."

His heart skipped a beat as he turned toward her, his heart pounding in anticipation.

"I know we shouldn't...but I can't ignore it anymore." She admitted, biting her lower lip nervously. "I have feelings for you."

Officer Norman swallowed hard, his throat suddenly dry. "I have them too," he confessed. "I've always had them, actually." They stared at each other for what seemed like an eternity before leaning in for a tender kiss. Their lips met softly at first, then eagerly as desire overtook them both. It was unlike anything they'd ever felt before. Their tongues danced together, exploring new territories as their hands roamed each other's bodies.

Finally pulling away, Officer Johnson whispered, "We can't let this consume us. What if it affects the investigation?"

Nate cupped her face in his hands, his thumbs grazing her cheeks gently. "I know but I don't want to lose you now that I've found you." He paused for a moment before adding, "Let's keep this a secret for now. Just us two."

She nodded, her eyes shining with unshed tears. "Okay," she whispered back. "Just us two."

From that day on, they worked hard to keep their relationship under wraps but their attraction to each other only grew stronger. They found small moments to steal away from the case—a lingering touch on the arm, a shared glance that spoke volumes—always careful not to let anyone else know about their newfound connection.

Their passion ignited in the car, on park benches, even during quiet moments of reflection. Every second spent together was electric, every touch sending waves of heat coursing through their bodies.

One night in particular remained etched in Nate's mind. They were on a stakeout at the abandoned warehouse where they believed Chosen had been last seen. The rain poured down outside, creating an almost symphonic rhythm on the rusty roof above them. They sat close together in the dark, watching the shadows play across the walls. The air smelled of damp and decay but all Nate could focus on was Johnson's sweet vanilla scent mingled with the cool night air.

"What if we forget about the case for just five minutes?" He whispered huskily into her ear, nibbling gently on it.

Johnson gasped, her heart racing. "What did you have in mind?"

Nate's hands found their way to her hips then up her shirt, trailing soft kisses along her collarbone. "I was thinking about how you taste," he murmured against her skin. "Like vanilla."

Her breath hitched as he captured her lower lip between his teeth, sucking gently. She pulled him closer, their bodies pressing tightly together. The adrenaline from the chase made things hotter than ever before.

As they made love against the cold concrete wall, thunder boomed outside, making it feel like fate's applause.

Now, back at the precinct, Officer Rebecca Johnson couldn't shake off the memory of that night. It seemed so long ago now. She couldn't believe she was actually dating her partner; it was both exhilarating and terrifying. Every time they shared a glance or brushed up against each other, her heart would skip a beat. They tried not to draw attention but sometimes failed miserably. Luckily, no one had caught on yet.

Detective Mitchell was going over the case files with them, his brow furrowed in concentration. He was getting closer to finding something, Nate could sense it.

Johnson wrote down notes diligently, her pen clicking against the paper. She glanced over at Nate every few minutes, their eyes meeting for just a moment before sliding away quickly. The taste of Nate lingered on her lips, minty from his gum.

The room was filled with the sound of paper shuffling and occasional sips from coffee mugs. Outside, rain tapped against the windows like tiny feet trying to get in. The case weighed heavily on everyone's minds.

Melissa Matthews sat alone at home, guilt eating away at her insides. She couldn't believe what she'd done, but she knew she had to protect her family. She couldn't lose them. She clutched a framed photo of her son, tears blurring her vision.

Across town, David Thompson was pacing the living room as Susan tried to calm him down. His heart ached for his son, Ted. What were the odds that Chosen would disappear shortly after Ted deciding to track his and Chosen's birth mother? He wished he could do more for Ted because he had not been acting like himself but knew they had to trust the police.

Chosen's house was eerily quiet without him; Natalie could hardly believe he was gone. She kept replaying their last conversation in her mind, searching for any clues as to what could have happened.

Officer Johnson squeezed Officer Norman's hand reassuringly, giving it a gentle squeeze before leaning in to whisper something in his ear. His stomach flipped at the smell of her perfume, sweet like vanilla. He nodded, taking a deep breath to steady himself. They both knew they had to keep going.

As Detective Mitchell left the room, Officer Norman felt a shiver run down his spine. He couldn't help but think about Ted—Chosen's twin brother.

Meanwhile, Susan Thompson drove home from running errands, her thoughts spinning. *What if they never find Chosen? What if he was gone forever? What are the odds Ted won't get to reunite with him?* She couldn't bear the thought. She pulled over to gather herself, taking deep breaths as rain pattered against the windshield.

Melissa Matthews brewed some tea at her home, trying to distract herself from the nagging feeling that something was off. The bustling town square seemed oddly deserted for this time of night. She took a sip of her drink, tasting its robust flavor. And then she saw it—a note tucked under her windshield wiper: 'Meet me at the lakehouse. Alone'. She froze momentarily, then contacted Officer Johnson.

Officer Johnson studied the map on her desk, her heart racing. The lakehouse was a long shot but it was worth investigating. She looked up at Nate, his eyes mirroring her own determination. He nodded and they both knew what they had to do: expose themselves to danger for the sake of finding Chosen.

The drive felt endless, the rain coming down harder now, blurring the windshield. Nate held his breath every time a car passed by, his knuckles white from gripping the dashboard. They finally arrived at the lakehouse, their hearts pounding in unison.

The place was eerily quiet, like something out of a horror movie. Officer Norman crept forward, his boots sinking into the muddy ground. Officer Johnson followed closely behind; her service weapon drawn. They were silent as they made their way inside, flashlight beams dancing across the walls. The stale air filled their lungs as they stepped into the musty living room.

The door slammed shut behind them, trapping them inside. Nate whipped around, searching for an exit as they heard footsteps approaching. Their hearts were a drumroll in their ears as they faced each other—a masked individual, holding a gun.

"You two shouldn't have come here," he growled, pointing the gun at them.

Nate felt a surge of protectiveness for Officer Johnson, not wanting her to be hurt. "We're here to help," he said, trying to reason with the man.

The man laughed maniacally, his eyes wild. "No one can help me now," he replied, moving closer to them.

Officer Johnson took a step forward, trying to reason with him too. "We don't have to do this. Let us help you and turn yourself in."

"I can't go to jail," he whispered fiercely. "It all slipped out of my control."

Fear rushed through Nate's veins. This was no longer about protecting anyone, it was about survival. He knew they had to act fast. Suddenly, he lunged forward, pushing Officer Johnson out of harm's way as a shot rang out, the wall behind him splintering from the impact. They both hit the floor hard, scrambling for cover. The smell of gunpowder filled the air.

The assailant was on the move again, trying to find them in the darkness. His footsteps echoed through the empty house.

Nate peeked around the corner, seeing movement outside. "Out the window!" He yelled, helping Officer Johnson to her feet and pushing her toward the exit. They dove into the rain-soaked grass, rolling away from the house. The cold water soaked their clothes, chilling them to the bone.

Another shot rang out, this one closer than before. They crawled through the muddy yard until they reached the road. Panting heavily, they looked back at the house. Smoke billowed from the chimney where flames began to lick at the walls. The house was ablaze.

"We did it," Officer Johnson whispered, looking at Nate with newfound respect in her eyes. "But we can't stop now. We still have to catch that man."

Chapter 8

The raindrops tapped an ominous beat against the foggy office window. Detective Mitchell hunched over his desk, pouring over the case files with tired eyes. The only light came from a single desk lamp, casting dark shadows across the room.

"We're getting close," said Officer Johnson, breaking the tense silence. She sat across from the detective, clutching a steaming mug of coffee. "The leads are piling up. Melissa's shaky alibi…this could be the break we've been waiting for."

Mitchell rubbed his temples, trying to ease the dull ache that had been plaguing him for days. "I know we're making progress," he said. "But it still does not feel like enough. We're running out of time."

Johnson leaned forward, her eyes bright with determination. "Hey, don't lose hope yet. We've got this. We'll find the truth."

The detective managed a small smile. He admired Johnson's optimism, even if he couldn't always match it. They sat in contemplative silence as the rain continued its persistent rhythm. Somewhere out there, the answers were waiting to be found. Mitchell just had to trust the process.

"You're right," he finally said. "Let's go over the timeline again. I know we're missing something."

The two hunched over the files once more, searching for the elusive clue that would break the case wide open.

The dim office fades away as the scene shifts to a rundown apartment on the outskirts of town. Clothes and takeout containers are strewn across the floor and the air is thick with stale cigarette smoke.

A disheveled man paces back and forth, muttering under his breath. This is Frank Douglas, his darting eyes and twitchy movements betraying his growing paranoia. He runs a hand through his greasy hair before lifting up the blinds to peer outside.

"They're onto us," he says to the two men sitting on the couch. Ted and Ethan exchange uneasy glances. They had trusted Frank to help them dispose of Chosen's body after a heated confrontation went too far. But now he seems volatile, unpredictable.

"Don't worry about the cops," Ethan says, trying to sound reassuring. "We were careful. There's no evidence."

Frank whirls around, his face contorted in anger. "Well, clearly you weren't careful enough! Why else would they keep sniffing around town, asking questions?" He resumes his frantic pacing.

Ted places a hand on Ethan's arm, a subtle signal to tread carefully. "Look, Frank," he says evenly. "We're all in this together. We just need to stick to the plan."

Frank pauses, considering this. After a moment, he nods reluctantly and takes a seat across from them. "You're right. We can't panic now," he says, lighting a cigarette with shaky hands. "We just need to lay low until this all blows over."

The three men sit in tense silence, the weight of their crime hanging over them like a dark cloud. They know the stakes if they're caught. But they're determined to protect each other, whatever it takes.

Ted watches Frank closely, noticing his jittery movements and darting eyes. Something seems off.

"What's really going on, Frank?" He asks. "You're acting strange. If you know something, you need to tell us."

Frank avoids their gaze, taking a long drag of his cigarette.

"I'm just worried, that's all," he mutters. "The cops are getting too close."

"We can handle the cops," Ethan interjects, leaning forward. "We just have to keep our cool."

Frank shakes his head. "It's not just the cops!" His voice rises in agitation. "I know people, okay? People who can make problems disappear."

He levels a pointed look at Ted and Ethan. "For the right price."

A tense beat passes. Ted feels his stomach drop, realizing the implication of Frank's words.

"You want us to pay you off?" Ethan asks incredulously.

Frank shrugs. "Hey, it's a small price to make this all go away."

Ted shakes his head angrily. "That wasn't the deal, Frank. We're supposed to protect each other."

"Yeah, well plans change," Frank snarls. "I'm putting my neck on the line here too. I think some compensation is in order."

Ethan scoffs. "No way. We had a deal." He looks to Ted for backup.

Ted feels trapped, his mind racing. Frank could expose them if they refuse. But giving in to his demands feels like a dangerous gamble.

Before he can respond, Frank stubs out his cigarette and stands abruptly.

"You've got 24 hours to think it over," he says coldly. "But don't take too long. My offer won't last forever."

He gives them one last threatening look before storming out, leaving Ted and Ethan stunned in his wake. They exchange anxious glances, both realizing the precarious position Frank has put them in. The betrayal cuts deep but they know he has them cornered.

For now, all they can do is wait and hope Frank doesn't make good on his threats.

Ted sinks into the chair, rubbing his temples as his mind spins. He had trusted Frank. Now it feels like the ground is crumbling beneath him.

"What do we do?" Ethan asks, panic edging his voice. "If we don't pay him, he'll go to the cops for sure."

Ted shakes his head, trying to think clearly through the adrenaline coursing through him.

"We can't pay him," he says finally. "It'll just make him keep demanding more. And we don't even know if we can trust him to stay quiet."

Ethan paces anxiously. "Yeah, but if we don't pay, we're screwed! He knows everything!"

Ted feels that same panicked sinking feeling. Frank has them cornered and he knows it. The power has shifted completely into his hands.

"There has to be another way," Ted says, desperation seeping into his voice. "Some other leverage we have on him. We just need time to think."

Ethan stops pacing, his eyes lighting up. "The security footage. From the bar that night. Didn't you say there's cameras in the alley?"

Ted's eyes widen. Security footage that would place Frank at the scene of the crime, right alongside them.

"Ethan, that's it," Ted says, a glimmer of hope cutting through the dread. "If we can get our hands on that footage, we'd have as much dirt on him as he has on us."

For the first time since Frank's confrontation, Ted feels like they have a shot at fighting back. The scales are tipping ever so slightly back in their favor.

Ted and Ethan share a look, the same thought passing between them.

"I'll handle it," Ethan says, a hardened expression on his face. "I'll get that footage, whatever it takes."

Ted nods, feeling a swell of gratitude for his loyal friend. "Just be careful. We can't risk you getting caught."

"I won't," Ethan says. "I'll get it done."

Ethan heads for the door, ready to embark on their only chance at freedom. But before he can leave, Ted grabs his arm.

"Ethan, thank you," he says sincerely. "I don't know what I'd do without you in all this."

Ethan gives a small smile. "What are friends for?"

With that, he disappears out into the night. Ted stands alone in the dim office, listening to the rain tapping rhythmically against the window. It mirrors the pulsing adrenaline still coursing through his veins.

They're not out of the woods yet. But now, at least they're fighting back. Ted takes a deep breath, mentally preparing for whatever comes next. The game is on.

The rain continues to patter against the office window as Ted stands alone, contemplating their next move. Frank's betrayal has left him shaken but also determined to regain control of the situation.

He thinks back to their confrontation with Frank earlier. The man had oozed a slimy arrogance, clearly relishing his position of power over them. Ted remembers Frank's beady eyes staring him down, his scraggly beard barely masking the smug grin on his face.

"You boys are in quite the mess, aren't you?" Frank had said, his voice dripping with contempt.

Ted had clenched his fists in frustration. Next to him, Ethan couldn't stand still, pacing anxiously around the small office space.

"What do you want, Frank?" Ted asked through gritted teeth. He already knew the answer but needed to hear the man say it himself.

Frank let out a raspy laugh. "What do I want? Let's see now…" He pretended to think about it. "How about enough money to set me up real nice in exchange for my silence?"

"You can't prove anything," Ethan blurted out, though the slight tremor in his voice betrayed his confidence.

Frank turned his beady eyes to Ethan. "Oh, I wouldn't be so sure about that…"

Ted remembers the sinking feeling in his gut at Frank's words. Of course, the man had leverage over them. Frank always seemed to be two steps ahead, a fact that filled Ted with frustration and rage.

But now, standing alone in the dim office, Ted feels the faintest sense of hope. If Ethan can get that security footage, they just might have a shot at fighting back. Ted knows it won't be easy but he has faith in his friend.

For now, all he can do is wait.

Ted paced the office, his footsteps echoing off the bare walls. The only light came from a single bulb hanging overhead, casting gloomy shadows across the room. He glanced at his watch, Ethan should've been back by now.

Worry gnawed at his insides. Had something gone wrong? Ted knew Ethan would have to get creative and that made him nervous.

The sound of the door opening snapped Ted from his thoughts. He turned to see a breathless Ethan, clutching a USB drive.

"Did you get it?" Ted asked urgently.

Ethan nodded, still catching his breath. "Wasn't easy but I managed."

Ted felt a rush of relief but it was short-lived. Now came the next problem—what to do with the footage.

"We need to destroy it, now," Ted said. He couldn't risk Frank obtaining another copy. This had to end here.

Ethan looked uncertain. "Are you sure that's enough? Frank knows about us, he could still talk."

"It's a risk we have to take," Ted replied. "Frank won't have any proof without this video. As long as we stick to our story, we should be okay."

He hoped he sounded more confident than he felt. They were running out of options and time. The investigation was gaining ground and soon their web of lies would unravel.

Destroying the footage was their only play left. Ted just prayed it would be enough to throw Frank off their trail for good.

Ted inserted the USB drive into his laptop with shaky hands. This was their chance to destroy the evidence implicating them in Chosen's death. If Frank somehow got his hands on a copy, it would ruin everything.

As the video file loaded, Ted's stomach churned. Watching the security footage again would be difficult but he had to confirm it was the right video before deleting it forever.

With Ethan peering over his shoulder, Ted pressed play. The video was in black and white and showed the parking garage near the alley on the night he had killed Chosen. It captured at a distance an unsuspecting Chosen after Ted appeared and struck him before dragging him off.

Ted tensed as he watched his twin brother's lifeless body hit the ground. The dark deed was done but the guilt still plagued him.

Ethan looked away, a pained expression on his face. "I can't watch this," he muttered.

Ted's cursor hovered over the delete button. This evidence had to be destroyed, no matter how hard it was to witness.

With a deep breath, he clicked delete. The progress bar crept along slowly as the file was permanently erased.

Ted leaned back, exhaling in relief. The video was gone. Without it, Frank had nothing on them. They were one step closer to getting away with murder.

Chapter 9

It was morning. With less than 12 hours remaining to meet Frank's ultimatum, Ted and Ethan sat in silence for a while, both lost in their own thoughts. The smell of coffee and burned toast filled the room as the server brought over their breakfast orders. Neither of them felt hungry but they knew they had to eat something to keep going.

"We need to move the body," Ted finally spoke, breaking the silence. "If the cops find it, we're both in deep trouble."

Ethan nodded in agreement; his mouth full of pancakes. He swallowed hard and said, "You're right. What do you suggest we do?"

Ted took a sip of his black coffee, his eyes darting around the small diner as if someone might be watching them. "We need to go back to that old abandoned warehouse where we hid him. I'll go in, get the body, and we'll take it somewhere else. This way, Frank doesn't know the location."

"But how are we going to move it without being seen?" Ethan asked skeptically.

"We'll figure something out," Ted replied, his voice firm. "We have to protect ourselves first."

They finished their meal quickly and made their way to the car, both feeling anxious and uneasy. The sun was just starting to rise, casting long shadows across the empty streets. As they drove to the warehouse, Ted's mind raced with possibilities while Ethan tried to calm his nerves with jokes and small talk.

The warehouse was a decrepit building on the outskirts of town, surrounded by overgrown weeds and rusted-out cars. It smelled of dust and decay as they entered, their footsteps echoing off the concrete walls. Ethan fumbled with his phone's flashlight while Ted led the way, feeling his way through the darkness. His heart pounded in his chest as he remembered the last time he was here.

When they reached the spot where they left Chosen's body, Ted knelt down, feeling the cold metal floor beneath him. He hesitated, taking deep breaths to steady his nerves. "Get some ropes," he whispered to Ethan, who left him momentarily to retrieve them from the trunk.

Together, they carefully lifted the heavy sheet of metal that concealed the trapdoor. The smell of earth and death wafted up, making Ethan gag. He covered his mouth and tried not to vomit as he watched Ted secure and lowered the rope to climb down into the opening.

The dim light from above barely illuminated the scene below. Ethan swallowed hard, trying not to think about what he was about to do. Ted lowered himself gently into the opening as Ethan shined a light. "I see the barrel," he said. Ted began to tie the rope around the barrel and yelled back to Ethan to begin pulling. With their combined effort, they managed to hoist the barrel containing Chosen's body parts out of the opening. Once Ted climbed out, they managed to load the barrel into the vehicle and drove off.

As they drove away from the scene with their grim cargo, Ted couldn't shake the feeling of foreboding weighing him down. Finally, they made their way back to Ethan's apartment where they collapsed onto the couch, exhausted but relieved. Ethan popped open a beer, the sound of the cap snapping off loud in the silence.

"What is our next step?" Ted asked, his voice hushed.

Ethan took a swig of beer, his throat dry. "At least Frank does not know where the body is anymore. We have to figure out where to put it." He glanced over at his friend, noticing how pale he looked. "You okay, man?"

Ted just nodded, unable to speak as he tried to process everything that had happened. They sat together in silence, listening to the cold air conditioner hum and the muffled city noise outside. Suddenly, a siren blared in the distance, growing louder by the second. Their hearts sank.

"Shit…" Ethan muttered. "It's too late now."

They both knew the police would be knocking on their door any moment.

With trembling hands, they dumped the tools and supplies into the duffel bag, trying to clean up as much evidence as possible before it was too late. They heard footsteps approaching and held their breath. The doorbell rang, echoing through the empty apartment complex.

"Let me do the talking," Ted whispered.

Ethan just nodded, his heart pounding like a drum.

Ted opened the door slowly, peering through the crack. Two uniformed officers stood there, their badges glinting in the dim light.

"We need to ask you a few questions," one of them said sternly.

"About what," Ted repeated dumbly.

"Chosen Matthews," the officer clarified. "We found his vehicle abandoned near an alley on the outskirts of town."

Ted froze. *Oh God...*

"I-I haven't seen him," Ted lied, trying to keep his voice steady. "Is there anything else I can do to help?"

The officers exchanged glances before one of them sighed. "No," he said. "But if you hear from him or know anything about his whereabouts, don't hesitate to call us."

As soon as they left, Ethan sagged against the doorframe. "Oh man...that was too close."

Ted's mind began to race. Maybe they could not pull this off without help, he thought. "Ethan, what should we do? This was a really close call."

Ethan agreed. His eyes darting around searching for ideas, he was afraid. "We destroyed the footage, right? At least now Frank has nothing on us, leveling the field." Ted was preparing himself for where Ethan was going with this.

"So, what?" Ted adds.

"Look," Ethan said finally, pausing to face Ted. "We need someone who's been through this kind of thing before. We need Frank."

Ethan knew Frank would be a hard sell. Frank had betrayed them in the past but they were running out of time and options.

"Frank?" Ted's voice was laced with disbelief. "You want me to trust the man who nearly ruined our lives? The man who lied to us, who manipulated us?"

"Look, I know it sounds crazy," Ethan admitted, rubbing the back of his neck anxiously. "But hear me out. He's got experience dealing with situations like this. He knows how to stay ahead of the police, how to cover his tracks. We need that kind of expertise if we're going to pull this off."

Ted's jaw clenched, his eyes narrowing as he weighed his options. He hated the idea of relying on Frank, especially after everything they'd been through. But what choice did they have? They couldn't keep running forever; eventually, their luck would run out.

"Fine," Ted conceded, his voice tight with frustration. "I'll contact him. But if he crosses us again, so help me..."

"Understood," Ethan agreed, his own apprehension mirrored in his gaze. "We can't afford any more mistakes."

"Then let's hope he's willing to help," Ted muttered, pulling out his phone and scrolling through his contacts. "Because if he isn't, we're out of options."

As Ted dialed Frank's number, a cold gust of wind whipped through the clearing, chilling him to the bone. It was as though fate itself was warning him of the consequences of their actions. But with no other viable options left, they had no choice but to forge ahead into uncertain darkness.

The sun dipped below the horizon, casting long shadows across the abandoned warehouse district. Ted and Ethan waited nervously in the dim light of a flickering streetlamp, a cold mist clinging to their breaths as they exchanged uneasy glances.

"Are you sure this is where Frank said to meet him?" Ted asked, rubbing his hands together for warmth.

"Yeah," Ethan replied, shifting his weight from one foot to the other. "But he's cutting it close."

Just then, the low rumble of an approaching car caught their attention. A sleek black sedan pulled up to the curb and Frank Douglas stepped out, his dark trench coat billowing behind him like a sinister cape.

"Sorry I'm late, boys," Frank said, a sly smile playing at the corners of his mouth. "Had to make sure we weren't followed."

"Can't be too careful, I suppose," Ted muttered, his distrust evident in his tone.

"Especially when dealing with someone like you," Ethan added, crossing his arms defensively.

"Fair enough," Frank conceded, nodding solemnly. "You agreed to pay me. Now, let's get down to business."

Frank led them through a maze of narrow alleyways until they reached a secluded spot, shielded from prying eyes by towering stacks of rusted shipping containers. As they huddled together, Frank began outlining his plan.

"First things first, we'll need to make sure the body is somewhere safe," Frank explained, his voice low and measured. "I've got a place in mind—remote, no nosy neighbors. From there, we can take our time cleaning up the scene, making sure we don't leave any loose ends."

Ted and Ethan exchanged wary glances, their uncertainty clear. "How do we know we can trust you, Frank?" Ted asked, his voice wavering slightly. "After everything that's happened, how can we be sure you won't turn on us again?"

"Look, I know I don't have the best track record," Frank admitted, running a hand through his silver-streaked hair.

"But this isn't just about me anymore. If we don't handle this right, all of our lives are at stake."

"Besides," he continued, his gaze meeting Ted's, "you two don't exactly have a wealth of options now, do you?"

'Trust' was a strong word, but as much as it pained them to admit it, Frank was right. They were backed into a corner and for the time being, they had no other choice but to rely on the man who had once betrayed them.

"Okay, Frank," Ethan said reluctantly. "We'll give this a shot. But if anything goes wrong, if you so much as think about double-crossing us, we're done."

"Understood," Frank replied, his eyes never leaving theirs. "You have my word."

As they shook hands, sealing their tenuous alliance, Ted couldn't help but feel a knot forming in the pit of his stomach. He knew they were making a deal with the devil, but at this point, it seemed there was little else they could do.

The sky was a dark canvas, intermittently illuminated by the flash of distant lightning. The air was heavy with the scent of rain and anticipation, a fitting atmosphere for what they were about to do. Ted's heart raced as he gripped the steering wheel tighter, his knuckles turning white.

"Alright, listen up," Frank began, unfolding a crudely-drawn map on the dashboard. "We need to get this done quick and clean. You'll find a remote location marked here," he pointed at a spot near the edge of town. "There's an abandoned well. We'll take Chosen's body there."

Ted glanced at Ethan, who looked equally uneasy. They shared a look of determination before nodding in agreement.

"Once we've got the body down the well, we'll fill it with concrete. It'll set quickly and no one will ever think to look there," Frank continued. "After that, we'll burn any evidence—clothes, personal items, anything that could link us to Chosen's death."

Ethan swallowed hard, his eyes betraying a flicker of fear. "And…what if something goes wrong?"

"Then we improvise," Frank replied, his voice steady and unnervingly calm. "But as long as we stick to the plan, we should be in the clear."

Ted forced himself to take a deep breath, knowing that their lives depended on executing this plan flawlessly. He couldn't afford to let his emotions get the best of him, not now. "Alright. Let's do this."

The three men exited the car, the wind picking up as they made their way to the trunk. As the storm drew nearer, the tension in the air became almost palpable.

"Help me lift," Frank ordered, gesturing toward the barrel. With great care, Ted and Ethan hoisted it up, doing their best to ignore the chilling reality of what they were holding.

As they trudged through the muddy terrain toward the abandoned well, Ted's thoughts were a whirlwind of guilt, desperation, and fear. He could feel the weight of not only Chosen's body but also the burden of their actions bearing down on him. But he couldn't afford to crumble, not when so much was at stake. He needed to stay focused, no matter how much his heart ached.

"Here it is," Frank announced, shining a flashlight onto the well's dark opening. "Get him in there and I'll start mixing the concrete."

Ted and Ethan lowered the barrel into the well as gently as possible, trying to ignore the sickening thud that echoed when he hit the bottom. As Frank busied himself with the concrete, the two friends shared an unspoken moment of grief and remorse.

"Alright, now we need to burn everything," Frank instructed, tossing them a canister of gasoline and a box of matches. "Be thorough. We can't leave any trace behind."

Ted took the gasoline and began dousing the area surrounding the well, while Ethan set fire to Chosen's belongings. The flames danced wildly in the darkness, casting eerie shadows across their faces as they watched the last remnants of their connection to Chosen's death disappear.

"Okay, it's done," Ted said, his voice barely audible over the roar of the fire. "Let's get out of here before anyone notices the smoke."

"Agreed," Frank replied, nodding solemnly. "From this point on, we stick together and we stay quiet. Understand?"

"Understood," Ted and Ethan murmured in unison, knowing that their fates were now irrevocably intertwined. As they made their way back to the car, the rain began to fall, washing away the last traces of the night's terrible events.

The rain pattered against the windshield, a constant reminder of the cleansing nature had just provided them. Ted gripped the steering wheel tightly as he navigated the winding back roads, trying to dampen the tremors that shook his hands. Beside him, Ethan stared out the window, lost in thought.

"Are you sure we covered everything?" Ted asked, his voice tense. "I can't shake the feeling we missed something."

"Frank outlined every step," Ethan replied, raking a hand through his damp blond hair. "We followed it to the letter. We should be in the clear."

"Should be isn't good enough," Ted snapped, his desperation seeping into his words. "If we're caught, it's not just our lives on the line. My family—"

"Hey, I know what's at stake," Ethan interjected, his own anxiety rising to match Ted's. "But panicking won't help us, Ted. We have to stay focused."

"Focused?" Ted scoffed bitterly, gripping the wheel even tighter. "How can I focus when every second brings us closer to discovery? The police, Natalie…they're closing in, and all we can do is hope our tracks are covered well enough."

"Look, I get it," Ethan said, turning to face Ted. "This is terrifying. But we've come this far and we did what we had to do. We can't change the past but we can control how we handle things in the future."

Ted glanced at Ethan, his eyes reflecting the fear and uncertainty that plagued his thoughts. He knew his friend was right but that didn't ease the heavy burden weighing on his chest—the knowledge that if they were caught, he'd dragged Ethan into a nightmare with no escape.

"Promise me one thing," Ted whispered, his voice cracking. "If it comes down to it, if they find out…save yourself. Don't go down with me."

"Ted—" Ethan began but Ted cut him off.

"Promise me, Ethan," he insisted, the desperation in his voice palpable. "Please."

Ethan hesitated, searching Ted's face for any sign of wavering. But he found only sincerity and a silent plea for reassurance. With a heavy sigh, he nodded.

"Alright," he murmured. "I promise."

As the car continued down the rain-soaked road, Ted couldn't help but feel an unbearable weight pressing down on him. He'd done what was necessary to protect his family but at what cost? If they were discovered, he would lose everything—including the one friend who had stood by him through it all.

But for now, they had no choice but to keep moving forward, their fates forever intertwined by the secrets they shared. And as the rain continued to fall, washing away the sins of the night, Ted knew that there would be no turning back.

Chapter 10

The sun hung low in the sky, casting an orange glow on the crumbling facade of the abandoned warehouse. Detective Mitchell pulled the car to a stop, gravel crunching under the tires. He and Officer Johnson stepped out, surveying the dilapidated building. Shattered windows gaped like missing teeth in the weathered brick walls, now covered in layers of graffiti. An eerie silence permeated the area.

"This is the place," Mitchell said gruffly. Johnson nodded, her gaze sweeping over the desolate landscape. She shivered despite the lingering warmth of the day.

Mitchell popped the trunk to retrieve supplies while Johnson secured the perimeter. She noted signs of transient activity—discarded food wrappers and cigarette butts. But deeper into the shadows, she spied a disturbance in the dirt.

"Over here," she called to Mitchell. He hastened to her side, shovel in hand. Together they stood over the suspicious item.

"Could be something," Mitchell muttered. He knelt beside it while placing on gloves. They shined their lights on it revealing the unmistakable shape of a body part: a finger.

Johnson paled, breath catching in her throat. "Could it be from Chosen?"

Mitchell's jaw clenched, sadness flickering in his eyes. "Poor kid. I hope not because he deserved better than this."

Johnson blinked back tears as she snapped photos, documenting every tragic detail. When forensics arrived, she and Mitchell stepped aside, hearts heavy with the weight of their discovery. But their work was far from over.

Mitchell watched solemnly as the forensics team carefully performed an examination. He felt a swell of sadness because it might mean the worst.

Johnson maintained a professional exterior but inside she was churning with emotion. It was always difficult in these situations because we can infer that someone's life took a violent turn.

The forensic investigators meticulously collected evidence from the scene. Fiber samples, soil samples, photos—nothing could be overlooked.

Mitchell knew the key now was the DNA evidence. Identifying whose body part lay before them would be crucial in determining what happened and maybe who was responsible.

As the finger was placed in a bag and loaded into the medical examiner's van, Mitchell turned to Johnson. "Let's get that to the lab right away. We need answers."

Johnson nodded, a look of determination on her face. They would get justice, no matter what it took. For now, the samples in their possession held the key to unraveling this tragic mystery.

Officer Johnson and Detective Mitchell worked efficiently as a team to collect any critical DNA samples.

Johnson carefully took notes while Mitchell used swabs to take samples of any potential blood. Their gloved hands worked swiftly and steadily, both detectives focused intently on the task at hand.

After sealing and labeling each sample, they stepped back and surveyed their work.

"That should be plenty for the lab to work with," Mitchell said, satisfaction in his voice.

Johnson nodded. "I'll get these shipped off right away. The sooner we can confirm the victim's identity, the better."

As Johnson headed for the car to retrieve the evidence shipping kit, Mitchell took one last look around. He felt they were one step closer to justice for the victim, though many questions still surrounded the case. Kneeling down, he scooped a sample of dirt into a small jar; it was always good to be thorough.

Securing the crime scene perimeter with police tape, Mitchell mentally reviewed the timeline of events leading up to this discovery. Chosen's disappearance, Melissa's odd behavior…something didn't add up. They were missing key pieces of the puzzle.

Johnson's return shook him from his thoughts. "All packaged up," she confirmed, holding up the sealed evidence box.

Mitchell nodded approvingly. "Good work today, Johnson. Let's get this shipped priority to the lab. I want those results as soon as possible."

As they headed for the car, Mitchell felt the familiar sensation of adrenaline pumping through his veins. The thrill of the hunt, of tracking down the truth. Justice was close, he could feel it.

Mitchell took a deep breath. Though he had seen many crime scenes in his career, it never got any easier. He steeled himself before kneeling down.

"If it was Chosen, poor kid," Johnson said softly as she snapped photos of the scene. "His whole life was ahead of him."

Mitchell nodded grimly. "Someone stole that from him. We'll make sure they don't get away with it."

Carefully, they logged the position of the body part and any identifiable features. This was no accident; someone had likely been murdered.

Johnson's camera flashed as she documented everything. Her usual lively banter was absent—out of respect, Mitchell knew. Despite her tough exterior, cases with potentially young victims always hit Johnson hard.

"Let's go give this person a name," he said. Johnson's eyes flashed with determination. They would find justice, no matter what it took.

Mitchell slid into the driver's seat as Johnson got in on the passenger side, letting out an exhausted sigh as she settled in.

"That was intense," she remarked, glancing over at her partner. "I know we've still got a long road ahead but I'm glad we finally found something. It feels like real progress."

Mitchell nodded slowly, staring ahead through the windshield for a moment before putting the keys in the ignition.

"I just hope the DNA results give us something solid to move forward with," he said. "We've been spinning our wheels on this case for too long."

He turned the key and the engine rumbled to life. As he pulled out of the parking lot, the light from the setting sun streamed in through the dusty windows of the worn-down warehouse behind them.

"I know we're both anxious to get those lab results back," Johnson said, "but try not to stress yourself out too much in the meantime. We've done good work today."

Mitchell managed a thin smile. "You're right. Let's just take it one step at a time from here."

He steered the car onto the main road, focused on the path ahead. Inside, his mind churned with speculation about where this investigation might lead next. But for now, all they could do is wait for the DNA evidence to expose the truth about the victim's identity. Wherever it takes them, they will follow the evidence until justice is served.

Chapter 11

Melissa sat at her kitchen table, staring at the pile of bills in front of her. The past due notices and eviction threats loomed over her like a dark cloud. She ran her hands through her shoulder-length wavy brown hair, feeling the weight of her financial struggle on her shoulders.

As she looked around the small, cramped place, her heart sank even further. The walls were thin, the paint was peeling, and the only furniture they had was a rickety old couch and a few mismatched chairs.

Melissa tried to shake off the feeling of despair and focus on her task: finding a way to survive. But as she scrolled through job listings on her laptop, her mind kept drifting back to the difficult decision she had made years ago.

Flashback to Melissa's past: She stood outside the hospital room, tears streaming down her face. She clutched onto one twin tightly while the other slept soundly in his bassinet. As much as it broke her heart, she knew she couldn't give both boys the life they deserved. So, in a warped yet idealized version of Sophie's Choice, with a heavy heart, she made the decision to give up one of her identical twin sons, Ted, for adoption and named the son she kept Chosen to remind her of the impossible choice she had to make.

The memory hit her like a ton of bricks and Melissa couldn't help but feel guilty. Did she choose to keep one twin, or did she really choose one twin to give away? She loved both of her sons with all her heart but circumstances forced her to make an impossible choice.

Back in the present, Melissa took a deep breath and pushed aside the memories. She had to focus on finding a job to keep a roof over her head and food on the table. But as she looked around at the cluttered house and thought about what her sons deserved, she couldn't help but wonder if she had made the right decision all those years ago.

Melissa sat at her kitchen table, surrounded by the remnants of a failed job search. She had been at it for hours, scouring the internet and making phone calls, but nothing seemed to work out. Her eyes were heavy with fatigue and her stomach grumbled in protest of yet another missed meal.

"Come on, Mel," she muttered to herself, scrolling through another job listing. "You have to find something."

But as she clicked through the endless pages of openings that required experience or credentials she didn't have, her mind began to wander. She thought about Ted, who was just a baby when she gave him up and whom she hoped was living a life of luxury with his new family. Each time a rejection email came through, Melissa couldn't help but feel guilty all over again.

"Excuse me, Ma'am?" A voice interrupted her thoughts.

Melissa looked up to see a middle-aged woman standing at her door. She wore a professional suit and held a clipboard, looking distinctly out of place among the eviction notices and piles of bills.

"Can I help you?" Melissa asked, rising from her seat.

"Hi, my name is Karen. I'm with the adoption agency that handled your son's case," the woman explained. "I wanted to check in and see how you're doing."

Melissa felt a wave of emotions wash over her at the mention of Ted. She hadn't heard from the agency in years and the sudden appearance of a representative caught her off guard.

"I'm fine," she said, her voice barely above a whisper. "Just trying to make ends meet, you know?"

Karen nodded sympathetically. "I can only imagine how tough it must be."

Melissa forced a smile but inside she was seething. Why did everyone assume that giving up one child meant she didn't care about him? She loved both of her sons fiercely but circumstances had forced her to make a decision that still haunted her to this day.

"Is there anything I can do for you?" Melissa asked, trying to keep the conversation brief.

Karen hesitated for a moment before speaking. "Actually, there is. We've been in touch with Ted's family and they're interested in meeting you in person."

Melissa's heart skipped a beat. The thought of facing the child she had given away was too much for her to bear. But at the same time, she couldn't help but feel curious about what kind of life he had led.

"I don't know," she said, her voice trembling. "I don't think I'm ready for that yet."

"Of course," Karen said quickly, sensing Melissa's discomfort. "It's entirely up to you. But just know that the offer is on the table."

As Karen left, Melissa sank back into her chair, her mind racing with conflicting thoughts. She didn't know what the future held, but one thing was for certain: the guilt and regret of her past decision continued to haunt her every day.

Flashback: Melissa sat nervously in the small office, her hands shaking as she clutched onto a crumpled tissue. The social worker across from her wore a kind smile but Melissa couldn't help feeling like she was being judged.

"Mrs. Matthews," the social worker began gently. "I know this is a difficult decision for you to make but I want you to know that giving up one of your sons for adoption could potentially provide him with a better life."

Tears streamed down Melissa's face as she thought about the choice she was being asked to make. She loved both of her boys equally and the thought of giving one of them away made her feel sick to her stomach.

"Can't I just keep them both?" She asked, her voice barely above a whisper.

"Mrs. Matthews, you're struggling financially, and the reality is that it will be difficult for you to provide for two children on your own. But if you were to give up one of your sons, he would have access to opportunities that might not be available to him otherwise."

Melissa looked down at the floor, her mind racing with conflicting thoughts. On one hand, she wanted what was best for her boys. But on the other hand, the thought of giving one of them away felt like a betrayal.

"Please take some time to think about this," the social worker said kindly, handing Melissa a stack of brochures about adoption agencies. "And know that we're here to support you, no matter what decision you make."

Melissa nodded numbly as she left the office, her heart heavy with the weight of her decision. As she walked home, she couldn't help but replay the conversation over and over in her head, weighing the pros and cons of each option.

She knew that giving up one of her sons would be the hardest thing she ever had to do. But deep down, she also knew that it might be the best thing for him. The thought of him growing up in a stable home with access to opportunities she couldn't provide made her heart ache, but at the same time, the guilt of giving him away would haunt her for the rest of her life.

Melissa's mind was consumed by her decision-making process as she entered her small, cluttered home. Bills and eviction notices littered the table, serving as a constant reminder of her financial struggles. She knew that something needed to change, and fast.

But for now, all she could do was pray that she was making the right decision.

The next day, Melissa sat across from the adoption agency representative, her hand shaking as she held the papers in front of her. The moment felt surreal, like she was watching herself from a distance.

"Are you sure about this, Melissa?" The representative asked, concern etched on her face.

Melissa took a deep breath and nodded, tears pricking at the corners of her eyes. "Yes, I'm sure. It's what's best for him."

The representative handed her the pen and Melissa signed her name on the dotted line. As she did, she felt a piece of her heart break off, knowing that she was giving up a part of herself forever.

But she also knew that it was the right thing to do. She couldn't provide the life that her son deserved, with all the opportunities and stability that he would have with his adoptive family.

As Melissa left the agency, she couldn't help but think back to that day so many years ago. The guilt still weighed heavily on her, even after all these years. Had she made the right decision? Would her son be better off with her?

She pushed those thoughts aside as she walked into her home. She smiled sadly, thinking of all the memories they had made together in a short period of time, and all the ones they would never get to make.

But despite the pain, Melissa knew that she had made the right choice. She believed Ted had grown up to be a wonderful young man. And although there were challenges along the way, he was happy and successful based on what she knows.

Melissa closed her eyes and whispered a prayer for her son, hoping that he was loved and happy. She knew that she had made the right decision all those years ago, even if it still hurt.

Flashback: Chosen walked down the street, his eyes scanning the rundown buildings that lined the sidewalks. The smell of sewage mixed with the scent of fried food from the nearby food carts. He saw children playing in the dirt and debris that littered the ground, their clothes tattered and worn.

This was the neighborhood where he grew up, where Melissa struggled to make ends meet after giving up Ted for adoption. Chosen's childhood had been filled with obstacles and hardships but he had learned to be resourceful and street-smart.

"Hey, Matthews!" A voice called out, and Chosen turned to see one of his old friends, Ty, approaching him.

"Hey, man," Chosen said, giving him a fist-bump. "What's up?"

"Not much, just hanging out," Ty replied. "You still working at that grocery store?"

Chosen nodded. It wasn't the most glamorous job but it paid the bills and allowed him to help support his family.

"Yeah, but I'm trying to find something better," he said.

Ty nodded, understanding. He knew all too well the challenges of growing up in this neighborhood.

"How's Ted doing?" Ty asked.

Chosen's expression darkened slightly at the mention of his twin brother. Ted had been adopted by a wealthy family and had grown up in a completely different environment than Chosen.

"He's doing fine," Chosen said shortly. "But we don't really talk."

"Damn, that sucks," Ty said sympathetically. "Must be hard not having your brother around."

Chosen shrugged but inside, he felt a pang of sadness. He had always wondered what his life would have been like if he had been the one adopted instead.

As they continued walking, Chosen couldn't help but contrast his own upbringing with Ted's comfortable life.

While Chosen had to scrounge and fight for everything he had, Ted had been handed everything on a silver platter.

But despite the differences in their upbringings, Chosen knew that they were still brothers and he would always have a connection to him.

"Thanks, man," Chosen said, clapping Ty on the back. "I gotta get back to work. See you around?"

"Definitely," Ty replied, waving as he walked away.

Chosen continued on his way, his mind focused on his goals and the future he wanted to create for himself and his family. He may not have had the same opportunities as Ted but he was determined to make his own path in life.

Flashback: "Ted, I'm sorry," Melissa had said tearfully as she signed the adoption papers. "I love you so much but I just can't provide for both of you and Chosen needs me more. He is sickly and needs more attention. I think you will have a better life with your adoptive family."

But present-day Ted couldn't understand what his birth mother had done. All he could feel was the resentment toward Melissa for giving him up, for not fighting harder to keep them together.

He stood up from the couch and walked over to the bar, pouring himself a stiff drink. He took a sip and felt the burn of the alcohol in his throat, momentarily distracting him from his thoughts.

But the bitterness remained. He had grown up with everything he ever wanted, but he still couldn't shake the feeling that something was missing. That he had been robbed of the chance to grow up with his twin brother.

"Damn it," he muttered under his breath, slamming the glass down on the counter. "Why did she have to do this?"

Meanwhile, Melissa sat alone in her small home, surrounded by the clutter of bills and eviction notices. The guilt of having given up one of her sons weighed heavily on her heart, even after all these years.

She had done what she thought was best for both of them but the pain never truly went away. She wondered if Ted ever thought about her, about their conversations and the decision she had made all those years ago.

"Would he hate me now?" She whispered to herself, tears welling up in her eyes.

She wiped them away and stood up, determined not to give up. She couldn't change the past but she could work toward a brighter future, hopefully.

As she gathered her things and headed out the door, Melissa couldn't help but feel the weight of her decision still bearing down on her. It would continue to shape her relationships, and the events to come in the story.

The click of the door lock announced their arrival at the safe house Frank had arranged. Ethan flicked on the light switch, revealing the cluttered room filled with old furniture and dusty knick-knacks. Ted gestured for him to close the door, then locked it behind them, bolting it for good measure. They both stood there, panting from their anxiety, their hearts slowing down to a more manageable pace.

Ethan collapsed onto a worn-out sofa and Ted joined him, the springs groaning under their weight. They sat in silence, sipping at the steaming mugs of tea Ted had gotten. The warmth of the beverage comforted them both as they stared at the screen of Ethan's laptop.

Just as they were about to begin, a loud thud shook the door, rattling its hinges. The two men exchanged worried glances. Ted carefully placed the laptop on a sturdy side table, reaching for the poker by the fireplace while Ethan grabbed a heavy vase from the coffee table, ready to defend themselves if needed. Slowly, they inched toward the door, their hearts pounding in unison.

With a loud crash, it burst open, revealing Frank, his eyes wild and desperate. He lunged at Ethan, tackling him to the ground and getting in a few shots. Ted sprang into action, as he dodged the man's clumsy blows. He landed a solid punch to Frank's jaw, sending him stumbling back. But Frank recovered quickly, snarling like a wounded animal. The room was suddenly filled with the sounds of grunts and thuds as they wrestled on the floor.

Frantic, Ethan scrambled for the phone on the end table, dialing for help. It was knocked aside as Frank slammed into it, sending it skittering across the wood planks. Suddenly, Frank reached for the letter opener on the desk, his hand closing around its cool handle. With a cold glint in his eye, he lunged at Ted, who barely managed to dodge the sharp blade. It cut through the air, narrowly missing his flesh.

Rage boiled up within Ted, replacing the fear that had temporarily paralyzed him. He grabbed Frank by the throat and pushed him against the wall, pinning him there. The room spun around him as he struggled to maintain his grip. Blood pounded in his ears, making it hard to think straight. All he could see was Ethan hurt and vulnerable, lying on the floor. Ted's hand clenched tighter around Frank's neck, cutting off his airway.

But then, a loud gasp escaped from Frank. His eyes rolled back into his head and he went limp in Ted's grasp.

With trembling hands, Ted released him, stepping back to catch his breath. Ethan staggered to his feet, his lip bleeding and eye swollen shut. They both stared at Frank, who lay unconscious on the ground, the metal letter opener protruding from his chest.

Together, they dragged him into the study and searched his pockets. Ted found a flash drive but there was no time to celebrate. Their hearts raced as they carefully considered options. They viewed the contents of the flash drive and found evidence linking Frank to Chosen and Melissa.

Apparently, they had dealings together and a history that preceded Chosen's death. "This is it," Ted muttered. "We can frame Frank for Chosen's disappearance and murder!"

Ted called for an ambulance concerned about Ethan. As the ambulance and police arrived, Ted helped Ethan to his feet. Ted gave one of the officers the flash drive that 'fell out' during the struggle. "We did it," he whispered. A wry smile twitched at Ted's lips as they watched Frank being wheeled away in a stretcher.

They rode together to the hospital in silence. Ethan's injury worsened as they sped through the city streets, his breathing becoming more labored and shallower with each passing moment. The pain medication made him drowsy but he refused to fall asleep. He held onto Ted's hand tightly, staring out of the window as they passed familiar places from their childhood—the park where they used to play baseball, the ice cream parlor where they celebrated their birthdays.

He couldn't help but feel a sense of loss for what could have been if things were different.

At the hospital, Ethan was admitted to the emergency room and Ted waited anxiously by his side. The nurses cleaned up his wound as best they could before running some tests. When Ethan finally fell asleep, Ted sat beside him. The beeping of the machines and sterile smell of the hospital filled the room.

Later that day, after Ethan was discharged with instructions to rest and recover at home, Ted took him to his place. They ordered pizza and watched old movies late into the night, processing the events of the day. Ethan's face still bore the bruises of the fight but there was an odd sense of satisfaction in their eyes. They survived Frank's assault, although they were unsure what prompted it.

In the morning, Ethan woke up feeling better but still weak from the ordeal. The sunlight streamed through the windows and painted Ted's face in warm hues as he made them both a pot of coffee. His fingers fumbled with the mugs, spilling a little milk on the counters as he tried to keep up with his emotions. He couldn't believe they had made it out alive.

Frank was in custody, his plan thwarted, and now Chosen's disappearance will be blamed on him. It was a surreal feeling that left him feeling both relieved and uncertain about what lay ahead.

They spent the day going through the evidence they'd collected at the office, piecing together clues about Frank's criminal activities. Ted felt a strange mixture of disgust and satisfaction as he discovered his brother's dark side and connection with Frank. He couldn't help but wonder if there were other secrets they hadn't uncovered yet. Nevertheless, the attention was on Frank now in connection with Chosen's disappearance and murder, not Ted.

As night fell, they decided to go for a walk the two of them alone in the quiet cemetery. It seemed fitting considering Chosen was gone. Ted couldn't help but feel regret. They sat there in silence for a long time, lost in their thoughts until Ethan broke it with a sigh. "I think we are officially detectives now," he said with a laugh that sounded more like a whimper.

Ted smiled weakly. "Yeah, who'd have thought?" They sipped their hot cocoa, letting the warmth spread through their chests as they stared up at the starry sky.

"To Chosen," Ethan murmured, clinking his mug against Ted's.

They finished their drinks and headed back to their car, leaving the cozy warmth of the night behind them.

The click of the car door opening echoed in the silent night air as Ethan entered and collapsed into the driver's seat, panting heavily. His breathing became even more labored as he tried to start the ignition but failed. "Ethan! What's wrong?" Ted asked, panic rising in his voice. Ethan's face paled, his fingers trembling on the keys. "I think…it's my side," he managed to say before passing out.

Ted frantically called for an ambulance while trying to stabilize his friend's position in the car. He unlocked the door and gently lifted Ethan out, cradling him like a baby as he waited for help to arrive at the cemetery. The cold air bit at his skin and he could hear the distant wails of sirens getting closer. Finally, a paramedic van pulled up and they rushed Ethan to the hospital.

Adrenaline surged through Ted's veins as they wheeled Ethan into the emergency room, Ted trailing closely behind. The beeping of machines and chatter of nurses filled the air, making him dizzy. He sank into a chair by Ethan's bedside, watching as doctors swarmed around him, checking vitals and asking questions. It felt like hours before one finally looked up at him.

"He's stable for now," the doctor said, "but we're keeping him overnight for observation. He has a few cracked ribs and internal bleeding we missed."

Ted let out a sigh of relief, rubbing his forehead wearily. He couldn't believe this was happening. What kind of twisted game was life playing with them?

Throughout the night, Ted stayed by Ethan's side, holding his hand and silently praying for his recovery. He ordered some food from a vending machine down the hall and brought it back to munch on while he waited; cold pizza and stale chips didn't taste nearly as good as usual. He couldn't shake the image of Chosen's lifeless body from his mind, nor could he forget the feeling of Ethan's body going limp in his arms.

When morning came, Ted decided to head home to get some rest. As he walked out of the hospital doors, he took one last look at Ethan, still asleep under the harsh fluorescent lights. The sun hit his face, making him squint as he stepped onto the busy sidewalk. People bustled past him, oblivious to his suffering. He hailed a cab home, climbing inside and collapsing into the seat, exhausted but unable to sleep.

It felt eerily quiet without Ethan there, like something was missing. He took a long hot shower, hoping to wash away the grime of the night before but it only served to remind him of the danger they had been in. Eventually, he fell into bed, his dreams filled with images of blood and death. After a short sleep, Ted got ready to return to the hospital.

The night was long and grueling for Ethan. He tossed and turned, his side throbbing from the injury. He knew it was bad but he couldn't recall much. Feeling nauseous, he managed to move enough to ask for water. A nurse brought him a cup and he sipped on it slowly, trying not to wretch at the taste of metal in his mouth. Every time he closed his eyes, he saw flashes of the altercation. The pain meds helped dull the ache in his side but did nothing for the emotional trauma.

As morning continued the hospital grew busier, Ethan drifted in and out of fitful sleep. A soft murmur caught his attention; someone was here. He cracked open an eye to see Ted sitting by his bed, holding his hand. He smiled weakly. "How long have you been here?" His voice was gravelly.

"Most of the night," Ted replied, squeezing his hand in reassurance. "Don't try to talk too much."

Ethan nodded, taking a sip of water. "You should go get some rest."

"I will, eventually," Ted promised. "But first, let me get you some real food." He left to fetch breakfast from the cafeteria, returning with eggs, toast, and juice. They ate quietly, neither wanting to discuss what happened yet.

As Ted left again, he felt a wave of guilt wash over him. It was his fault they were in this mess. He had brought Ethan into this world of crime and danger and now his friend could have been killed. What if he didn't make it? The thought made him shiver uncontrollably.

The next few days were a blur of doctors' appointments and waiting rooms. Ethan's parents visited, their faces etched with worry, thanking Ted for his help. But that only made him feel worse. The stern nurse gave him an ultimatum: leave or be arrested for trespassing if he didn't have a room. Each night, Ted sneaked back into the hospital to check on Ethan, always finding a different nurse on duty but never leaving his side.

On the third day, Ethan was discharged, looking pale and weak. Ted filled him in on what he knew. They agreed it was best to keep their heads low until things cooled down. As Ethan gathered his things, he turned to Ted. "Thank you," he said quietly, looking vulnerable for the first time since childhood.

Ted blinked away sudden tears. "I couldn't let you die," he replied gruffly. They drove home in silence, both lost in their own thoughts. When they arrived at the house, Ted realized something was off; it was too quiet. They crept inside to find the place empty.

Ted tried to focus on cooking dinner but the smell of burned eggs only made him more jittery. They ate in silence, avoiding each other's gazes. As night fell, they heard a knock on the door. Ted hesitated, then answered it. It was Detective Mitchell, Officer Johnson, and Melissa.

After exchanging greetings, he invited them inside. "With the person responsible for Chosen's disappearance in custody, I never had a chance to check on you and say thank you," Melissa said.

"No need, I'm fine," said Ted.

"You look so much like Chosen, it is uncanny," Melissa remarked. "Chosen would have loved to reunite with you; if not in this life, then the next."

The authorities believed that Frank had killed Chosen and attacked Ted because he wanted to hurt Melissa for defaulting on a debt she owed. They have no idea of their real connection, however.

Chapter 12

Ted Thompson stood alone in his room, the silence weighing heavily on him. He could hear his own breaths echoing in his ears as he paced back and forth, his thoughts racing. The DNA test results were due any day now and he was consumed by the weight of his actions.

"Should I turn myself in?" Ted muttered to himself, running a hand through his hair. "What about Ethan? What will happen to him if I do?"

The image of his childhood friend flashed through his mind, his carefree smile and infectious laughter. Ted sighed, knowing that Ethan's unpredictable nature would only make things more complicated.

"Maybe I should just keep running now that Frank is in custody," Ted thought aloud, continuing to pace. "But for how long? I can't live like this forever."

He paused by the window, gazing out at the city below. Memories flooded his mind, both good and bad. The day he found out he was adopted, the anger he felt toward Melissa for giving him up. But also the love and stability he found with his adoptive parents, who had given him a home and a family.

"Who am I?" Ted whispered, struggling with his identity. "Am I the same person as Chosen, or someone completely different?"

He shook his head, the exhaustion of his internal debate taking a toll on him. Ted needed to find some solace, a quiet place where he could reflect on his decisions and find clarity.

"Maybe I'll go to the park," Ted said to himself, making a decision. "I need some fresh air."

With a deep breath, Ted left his room and headed outside, unsure of what the future held.

Ted stepped into the park, his eyes scanning the area for an empty bench. He spotted one by a small pond, surrounded by trees and chirping birds. As he walked toward it, he couldn't shake off the feeling of guilt that gnawed at his insides.

"Was turning myself in the right thing to do?" Ted muttered, sitting down on the bench. "What will happen to Ethan, Melissa, and my parents?"

He rested his elbows on his knees, burying his face in his hands. The weight of his actions felt suffocating and he struggled to catch his breath.

"Think, Ted," he whispered to himself, trying to calm his racing thoughts.

He closed his eyes and let his mind wander back to his childhood. To the day he found out he was adopted, and the anger he felt toward Melissa for giving him up. But also the love and stability he found with his adoptive parents, who had given him a home and a family.

"Am I really capable of hurting someone?" Ted wondered, his heart heavy with guilt.

"Chosen was always the better one," Ted mumbled, tears streaming down his face. "The one with the kind heart and pure intentions."

But as much as he admired his brother, Ted knew he could never be like him. He was too consumed with his own desires, his need for control and stability.

"Maybe that's why I should turn myself in," Ted said aloud, wiping away his tears. "To prove to myself that I can be better. That I can make amends for my mistakes."

He took a deep breath, feeling a sense of clarity wash over him. The decision was made and he knew what he needed to do.

"I will not let Chosen's death be for nothing," Ted said, standing up from the bench and heading back toward his room.

Ted collapsed onto his bed, exhausted both physically and emotionally. He stared up at the ceiling, his mind racing with questions he couldn't answer.

"Who am I really?" He whispered to himself, a sense of emptiness settling in his chest. "Am I just a product of my environment? Or can I change who I am?"

He thought back on his life, from his troubled childhood to his successful career as a lawyer. But despite all his accomplishments, he couldn't shake the feeling that something was missing.

"Is this what redemption feels like?" He asked himself, the weight of his actions finally taking a toll on him. "Is it worth sacrificing everything for?"

He closed his eyes, trying to block out the doubts and fears that plagued him. But they kept creeping back, tormenting him with their relentless persistence.

"Maybe I should have never come here," he said aloud, the words sounding hollow even to his own ears.

But he knew deep down that he couldn't run from his past forever. He had made mistakes but he was still capable of doing good.

"Redemption is a choice," he said firmly, sitting up and looking around his room with renewed determination. "And I choose to do what's right."

With that, Ted got up from his bed and began packing his bags, ready to face whatever consequences awaited him. The road ahead would be difficult but he knew that he had to take the first step toward redemption.

Ted stepped out and took a deep breath of the cool, crisp air. The sun was just beginning to set, casting a warm glow over the city. He needed to clear his head to find some clarity amidst the chaos that had consumed his life.

He walked aimlessly, his thoughts racing as he weighed the pros and cons of turning himself in. If he went to the authorities, he would be admitting to a crime that could potentially destroy his career and his relationships with his loved ones. But if he continued to hide, the guilt and fear would continue to eat away at him until there was nothing left.

As he wandered, Ted found himself in a quiet park, surrounded by the rustling of leaves and the distant sounds of traffic. He sat down on a bench, his mind still churning with conflicting emotions.

"Is this really what I want?" He muttered to himself, his eyes fixed on the ground. "To spend the rest of my life looking over my shoulder, always wondering when they'll catch up to me?"

He shook his head, trying to push the thoughts away. But they kept coming back, gnawing at his conscience like a persistent itch.

"Maybe it's time to come clean," he said aloud, the words sounding foreign to his own ears. "To face the consequences of my actions and try to make things right."

The thought both terrified and exhilarated him. He knew that he would have to give up everything he had worked for, but maybe that was the price of redemption.

"Or maybe I'm just being foolish," he muttered, the doubts creeping back in. "What if they never forgive me? What if I lose everything?"

But then he remembered Melissa, the woman who had given him up for adoption all those years ago. She had made a difficult choice, one that had undoubtedly changed the course of her life. Maybe it was time for him to make his own difficult choice.

"Melissa was brave enough to give me a chance at life," he said, his voice growing stronger with each word. "And now it's my turn to be brave."

With that, Ted stood up from the bench and began walking back. He knew that the road ahead would be difficult but he was ready to face it head-on.

Ted sat alone in his study, surrounded by piles of paperwork and stacks of books. The only sound was the ticking of the antique clock on the wall, counting down the minutes until the DNA test results would arrive.

His heart raced as he thought about what the results could reveal. Would they confirm his worst fears? Or would they bring some small measure of relief?

He picked up a pen and began doodling absently on a sheet of paper, trying to distract himself from the looming uncertainty.

"Come on, Ted," he muttered under his breath. "You're a grown man. You can handle whatever comes your way."

But the fear of losing everything he had worked so hard for gnawed at him like a hungry beast. He couldn't bear the thought of being stripped of his identity, his career, his relationships.

And yet, the guilt of his actions weighed heavily on him. He knew that turning himself in was the right thing to do but the consequences were too great to ignore.

"Maybe I should just run," he said aloud, the words echoing through the empty room. "Disappear somewhere far away, start over."

But he knew that was a coward's way out. He had to face the music, no matter how difficult it might be whether that music meant turning himself in or the guilt of getting away with murder.

As the minutes ticked by, his thoughts grew more frantic. He paced back and forth across the room, his mind racing with conflicting emotions.

"I can't do this," he said, his voice shaking with fear. "I'm not strong enough."

But then he remembered Melissa, the woman who had given him up for adoption all those years ago. She had believed in him even when he didn't believe in himself.

"Melissa wouldn't want me to give up," he said firmly, his resolve strengthening. "She would want me to fight, to face the consequences of my actions."

With a deep breath, Ted sat down at his desk and waited for the DNA test results to arrive. Whatever they revealed, he knew that he would face them head-on, with courage and determination.

Ted sat in his car, the engine idling softly beneath him. He stared out at the street, watching the cars pass by with a hollow sense of detachment.

He had been driving around for hours, trying to clear his head and come to a decision. But the more he thought about it, the more confused he became.

"Damn it," he muttered, slamming his hand against the steering wheel. "Why is this so hard?"

He knew that turning himself in was the right thing to do. He couldn't keep living like this, always looking over his shoulder, always waiting for the police to catch up with him. But the thought of losing everything he held dear—his freedom, his family, his relationships—was almost too much to bear.

"Maybe I'll just keep driving," he said aloud, half-jokingly. "Start a new life somewhere else."

But he knew that was a fantasy. He couldn't keep running forever. Sooner or later, he would be caught, and then everything he had built would come crashing down.

"Okay," he said, taking a deep breath. "Time to face the music."

With a firm resolve, Ted put the car into gear and drove toward the police station. As he walked through the doors, his heart pounding in his chest, he knew that there was no turning back.

"Excuse me," he said to the officer at the front desk. "I need to talk to Detective Mitchell, please."

The officer raised an eyebrow but didn't seem particularly surprised.

"Name?" He asked, pulling out a clipboard.

"Thompson," Ted said. "Ted Thompson."

The officer nodded and jotted down the name.

"Take a seat," he said, gesturing toward the waiting area. "Someone will be with you shortly."

Ted sat down on one of the hard plastic chairs, his hands shaking with nerves. He closed his eyes and took a deep breath, trying to calm himself down.

Okay, he thought, his mind racing. *This is it. This is the moment of truth.*

The minutes ticked by like hours as he waited for someone to come and take him in. He could feel the weight of his actions bearing down on him, crushing him under its heavy burden.

Am I doing the right thing? he wondered, his thoughts spiraling out of control. *What if this is all a mistake? What if I'm making things worse?*

And then the door opened and a police officer stepped into the waiting room.

"Mr. Thompson?" She said, her voice professional but kind. "It's time."

Ted stood up slowly, his heart beating so loudly he could hear it in his ears. He took one last deep breath, then followed the officer out of the room.

Chapter 13

Ted sat alone as he waited for Detective Mitchell to come in. His mind running over what he was going to say, Ted thoughts were interrupted by a knock at the door before Mitchell entered. "So, what brings you here?" Mitchell asked.

Ted's palms were clammy from anxiety. "I have to help put things right," he said. "If the man who attacked Ethan and me was involved in Chosen's disappearance, I want to do whatever I can to make sure justice is served."

Mitchell was sitting in his chair leaning back with his arms folded across his chest taking a moment to digest Ted's words. "Well, it turns out that the flash drive he was carrying contained incriminating evidence linking him with your twin brother, Chosen, and Melissa." Ted let out a slight sigh. "Right now, Frank remains in custody under suspicion for Chosen's disappearance," Mitchell continued. Ted had to control his reaction so as not to reveal anything.

"If it is beneficial for me to be used as a witness to help the case for Chosen, then I am willing to cooperate," Ted mentioned.

"Frank has cooperated with us telling us where Chosen's body is in exchange for leniency. Although he has not confessed to the murder, he will be going away for a long time," explained Mitchell. "Frank actually tried saying that you killed Chosen but since there is no evidence or motive for such a story, the case is closed."

Detective Mitchell got up and left the room, leaving Ted alone again. Ted decided that Frank deserved to be where he was. Frank had tried to double-cross him before. Surely Frank had done some really horrible things in his day; this is justice for those things.

What happened to Chosen was not premeditated and Ted never meant for it to happen. Besides, he had suffered and lost everything—turning himself in would benefit no one.

Ted stood up and walked out of the room slowly. As he headed toward the exit, he could not help but to think of all of the events that had transpired. It had been more than anyone should have to go through.

Stepping outside the station doors, catching a glimpse of David and Susan in the distance, he muttered to himself, "Time to live the life that my mom would have wanted for me." The corners of his mouth slowly curled into a smile as he walked down the steps toward David and Susan, never to look back.

It was odd he chose to use the word 'Mom'. Ted never referred to Melissa as his mom, nor Susan. The only person who referred to anyone as mom was…Chosen.

Considering what we know of the twins, sure Chosen was street-smart but Ted was the twin always in control. So, it does not make sense that he would lose his temper and Chosen be the one in control. According to what happened, each was behaving like the other in the alley and actions speak louder than words.

As it turns out, in the alley the night of the murder, Chosen was the aggressor, striking Ted with the brick killing him. Immediately after striking Ted and dragging him off to the dumpster, Chosen switched jackets with Ted because they were both wearing jeans at the time.

The rain had wet Chosen's hair and Ted's which was similar in length. Chosen then pretended to be Ted and told Ethan a lie about what happened, just switching the names. Ethan probably did not question anything because the nature of the events that took place were possible, though perhaps unexpected.

Ethan inadvertently fed Chosen as Ted the information he needed to fill the knowledge gaps about Ted's life facilitating the impersonation. Even though Frank Douglas never let on that he knew Chosen all along, both him and Ethan thought they had dismembered Chosen's body while Chosen as Ted, knew they were actually dismembering Ted's body.

Since they were identical twins, genetics would be identical as well. The only distinguishing features between the twins are their biometric traits. However, only DNA was used to confirm identity of Chosen because there were no officially documented biometric traits to confirm identity.

Chosen had been the one to kill his twin brother and assumed his life to preserve his own. His mother, Melissa, had talked about Ted to him while growing up, which is how he knew of Ted. Thanks to what Melissa had shared with Chosen, he was jealous of Ted and immediately took advantage of the situation when an opportunity presented itself.

Why did Ted get to have a wonderfully privileged life while Chosen struggled every day? So, the moment the opportunity presented itself, Chosen capitalized.

Chosen had followed Ted. It was Chosen who had signaled for Ted to pull over. It was Chosen who led Ted into the alley he selected. Chosen had been the one orchestrating everything. Chosen was so convincing as Ted that Frank Douglas, who never let on that he knew Chosen, did not even know he was, in fact, dealing with Chosen when they asked him for help initially.

Eventually, however, Frank must have figured out Chosen was impersonating Ted and that is when he came to the safehouse, furious, and attacked him. Fortunately for Chosen, Frank's credibility was terrible, so framing him for the disappearance of his brother was easy. Now, in his new life as Ted, he will have to adjust somewhat. Nonetheless, the real Chosen gets to live the life he's always dreamed of and one that he feels is rightfully his.